LEE TANNER

Phillip Underwood

Walker and Company
New York

To the memory of my father,
Oran William Underwood

First published in the United States of America in 1989 by Walker Publishing Company, Inc.

Published simultaneously in Canada by Thomas Allen & Son Canada, Limited, Markham, Ontario

Library of Congress Cataloging-in-Publication Data

Underwood, Phillip.
Lee Tanner / Phillip Underwood.
p.   cm.
ISBN 0-8027-4099-5
I. Title.
PS3571.N438L4   1989
813'.54—dc20   89-34602
CIP

Printed in the United States of America

10 8 6 4 2 1 3 5 7 9

CHAPTER 1

NO horse could buck its way through drifts four and five feet deep for long, no matter how much heart, and the big roan Appaloosa that Tanner rode could keep going longer than most. But Tanner was first a horseman, and he treated any animal he chose to ride with respect. So, while Tanner was not particularly cold or tired himself, it was because of his horse Jake that he left the main trail and fought his way through the snow to the cabin sheltered beneath the blue spruce. And were it not for Lee Tanner's respect for horseflesh, the old man Tanner found in the cabin would have died alone.

When Tanner entered, he saw the old man lying on the bunk in the corner, an arm draped across his eyes. The smell was overwhelming—feces and urine, wet ashes in the fireplace, and sour, unwashed clothes and body.

The old man moaned softly, and Tanner knew death for the old cowhand could not be far away.

The least he could do was make the stranger as comfortable as possible. With that in mind, Tanner set about building a fire in the old stove and putting water on to heat. When the cabin was warm and the water hot, he cleaned the old man as best he could, sponging away the filth and restoring a little color to the flesh. He made for him a fresh bed in one of the other bunks, using his own bedroll, and then lifted the wasted body onto it, wrapping the blankets close.

After a time the pale eyes fluttered open, darted about in animal-like fear, and then focused on Tanner's face. With recognition came a peaceful smile.

"Well, friend," the man whispered. "Looks like you hove

1

up just in time fer the last waltz." A wistful smile pulled at the blue lips. "Seein' as how you're goin' to be holdin' my hand and marchin' me up to them gates, we might as well be innerduced. Clay Barstow's the name. Friends call me Rooster."

Tanner took a gentle grip on the emaciated right hand. "Lee Tanner. Pleased to meet you. What's the trouble, old-timer? You look like you've been bucked off and kicked pretty good."

"Pneu-mony, I believe," wheezed Rooster. "I got myself good 'n' wet in the storm, an' then damn near froze my butt off—lungs were ruint when I was a youngster in the coal mines."

Tanner nodded. Pneumonia. That would fit, all right: the congested rattle in the lungs—the burning fever.

The old man smiled, and then his eyes squinted in thought. "Tanner," he muttered. "You wouldn't be kin to Dobie Tanner, from Denver?"

Tanner thought a moment. "My folks hail from west slope, down around Ouray."

"Maybe a cousin or sumpin', huh?"

"Maybe," he said agreeably. "I got a pitiful concoction I call stew over there, Rooster. Reckon you could handle a cup of it?"

"I could try. If it's like my ma used to make, it just might take care of what ails me."

Tanner took a duffel bag and fashioned it into a pillow to prop up the old man's head and shoulders.

The stew was scalding hot, so Tanner added a little cold water. He cradled Rooster's head in his left arm and held the tin cup to his lips.

One swallow. And then another. The old man gagged, went into a spasm of coughing that left him gasping, unable to speak for several minutes.

Finally Rooster croaked. "Hate to break it to you, son. That stew of yourn ain't nowheres as good as my ma's. Matter o' fact, it may have just drove the last nail in my coffin lid. I think I had me a fightin' chance until I et that." A mischievous light glittered in the pale eyes.

Tanner smiled. "I got me a favor to ask of you, Tanner." Rooster's eyes grew serious. "A big favor."

"Ask away, ol' pard," said Tanner softly.

"I work for the Triple T. First place you come to when you hit the flats. I got no desire to spend the winter layin' here in this infernal cabin. An' you put me outside, the wolves'll eat me fer dinner. You reckon when it's over, you could put me on ol' Blossom out there and take us both down to the ranch? That'll leave them the chore of buryin' me. Their fault I'm out here anyhow." He raised a frail arm and let it fall back to his side. "Too old to be out brush poppin' in the dead of winter anyhow. Plenty of younger men fer that . . . Too old an' too goddamn tired . . ."

His lips moved without sound. Tanner leaned close, and the old man's words, heavy with the smell of death, came through. "Tell Eleanor," he whispered, "that it's all over. She's to rest now. She don't have to worry no more."

Rooster's eyes drifted closed. Tanner could detect no breathing. He placed a hand next to the heart and felt only a timid flutter. In a moment that, too, faded away to a stillness as deep and as lonesome as the old cabin itself.

Tanner rose stiffly, looking down at the tired old face, now relaxed and at peace.

"Rest easy, Rooster," he said softly. He pulled the old army blanket up to cover the dead man's face.

Suddenly it seemed to Tanner the cabin had taken on a new chill. He threw a few more sticks into the stove and, leaving the coal oil lamp burning for the extra heat, threw himself on the rawhide webbing of the nearest bunk and fell immediately unconscious. As he spiraled down into the blackness of sleep, one name floated up to him from the depths. "Eleanor," he mumbled.

* * *

First light arrived shrouded in a gray mist. It found Tanner roping the old man's body, encased mummylike in Tanner's bedroll, across the mare's saddle. The air carried a sharp snap, and a thin crust of ice from the freezing mist glazed the surface of the snow.

Tanner's ears and nose were numb and his fingers were stiff and clumsy as he knotted the rope around the body. When he finished, he struggled into his elk-hide gloves and beat his arms briskly against his side, working a little warmth into his chilled frame. He regretted now not taking the time for a fire. But it was his hope that with an early start he might make it down into the valley and to shelter before nightfall.

It was tough going. Two hours later, he stopped to rest the horses beneath a rock overhang. Protected from the snow, the ground was dry and showed signs of a recent camp. Tanner matched the hoofprints he found with those of Rooster's mare and decided here had been the old man's last camp before holing up in the cabin. Since the snow around the overhang had been unbroken before Tanner's arrival, he guessed that the old man had been at the cabin for quite a spell, at least several days. Going by the weakened condition of the mare, he also surmised that Rooster must have been incapacitated to the point of being unable to care for the animal much of the time.

With a thought to building a small warming fire, Tanner began searching for bits of wood in the cleared area beneath the overhang. At its edge, portions of a deadfall protruded from beneath the heavy blanket of snow. There he found several dried branches and twigs, and he had broken off a plentiful supply when he spotted the horse's hoof—shod, with ice particles clinging to the worn metal of the shoe.

Perplexed, he lifted a few of the branches and dislodged enough of the snow to disclose a reddish, ice-encrusted flank. The gleam of a buckle caught his eye, and he found a girth strap, still cinched tightly in place.

He worked with a will, clearing away the remainder of the deadfall. Sometimes horses died and were left by their owners for the wolves. Never had Tanner seen one left with full rigging—saddle, saddle pad, and bridle.

When he finished freeing the dead animal from its ice tomb, Tanner viewed the remains of an exceptionally fine sorrel gelding. It looked to be a fairly young horse, and sound, as far as Tanner could tell. No sign of a broken leg or any other injury. No reason at all to explain the single round bullet hole in the center of the horse's forehead.

He stood in the cold and pondered, the fire forgotten.

"What the hell?" he asked aloud, and the sound of his own voice startled him.

There must have been another rider who arrived at the overhang either before or after (or at the same time as) Rooster. What had happened to him? If Rooster had seen him, why hadn't the fellow helped the old man? Or if the fellow had needed shelter, why had he not made the cabin with Rooster? If he was dead . . . Tanner shook his head.

The horse had been deliberately shot, that much was for certain. And an attempt had been made to hide the carcass until the wolves could dispose of it permanently.

Another thing—why had no one from the Triple T come searching for the old man? Of course, the frequent heavy snows up in the high passes would hamper any search effort and make it extremely dangerous for any man to go out. One such storm could wipe out in ten minutes all traces of a man's tracks.

Tanner turned and regarded the weakened little mare with its sad burden. He shrugged. With a final glance at the dead horse, he turned and mounted. The Appaloosa again began breasting the deep, crusting drifts as the mare struggled on, fighting gamely in the wake of the big horse.

The going got easier more quickly than Tanner had hoped. He had crested the pass. The timber gave way to sparse groves of quaking aspen and patches of Oregon grape, and, below that, flinty ridges of bare, windswept rock. Buffalo grass poked through the snow here and there, and Tanner saw signs that large numbers of deer and elk had been feeding here. Little game moving about indicated another storm might be brewing, so he quickened his pace.

By midafternoon, he had reached the flats, where only a skiff of snow covered the brown grass. The heavy, freezing mist continued, however, and Tanner was relieved, as darkness approached, to see lights a short distance ahead.

The mare stumbled, staggered, but caught itself and remained on its feet.

"Hang on, old girl," encouraged Tanner. "We damn near got it made."

The mare jumped wildly at the reins in Tanner's hand. At the same instant, a rifle shot crashed about him.

There was a rush of hooves, and Tanner pulled his rifle from the scabbard.

"Leave it be, mister." Three dark forms closed in, and Tanner found himself surrounded. "Lest you want to be draped 'cross your saddle like your friend there."

The speaker was a heavy figure, shrouded in a greatcoat, a wool stocking cap pulled low over the ears. Tanner could see in the gloom only a blur of features—a wide flat nose, drooping mustache. The man held a rifle across the pommel, directed at Tanner's middle. Behind him and to one side were two more specters, each with leveled six-gun.

"First things first," said the big man. "Your name." It was not a question but a command.

"Who's asking?" Tanner worked his free hand under his sheepskin coat.

"I'll ask one more time. An' then you're leavin' that saddle." There was no mistaking the man's tone. No bluff, no threat. Simple statement of fact.

"Name's Tanner."

"Who's that under wraps?" The big man used the rifle as a pointer, indicating the body.

"Told me his name was Barstow." Tanner eased his hand from under his coat. He would have to go along for now. The odds were just too heavy against him. "Found him in a cabin up on the pass."

"Was he dead when you found him?"

"How the hell could he tell me his name if he was dead?"

"Mister." The big man's voice was deadly. "Maybe you just don't realize how serious I am about all this."

Tanner shrugged. "He was bad sick. Appeared to have a bad case of pneumonia. Just barely alive. He couldn't talk much—too far gone. Told me who he was and asked me to bring him down off the mountain. Said he worked for the Triple T."

There was a moment of silence while the big man seemed to digest the information. The horses stamped and blew—otherwise, save for the wind, all was still.

"That's all he said?" the rifleman asked finally. "Didn't happen to say what he was doing up there?"

"Brush poppin'. Looking for late strays. I figured he got too far out. Maybe got caught in the storm, come down sick, and figured he was too weak to make it back."

Tanner was on the point of revealing his finding of the dead horse when wariness, or stubbornness, stilled his tongue.

One of the men behind Tanner put spurs to his horse's flanks and wheeled the animal about where he could peer into Tanner's face. "Tanner, huh? Ain't I seen you someplace before? You on the run?"

Tanner could not see the man's face clearly in the gloom, but the voice was young and full of challenge. The man motioned carelessly with his six-gun.

Tanner said calmly, "Where I'm from, we don't question a man too much about his past. Least not with a gun in your hand."

There was a tense moment, and the big man spoke. "Back off, Billy. I'm handlin' this." He turned to Tanner. "Well?"

Tanner relaxed in the saddle, both hands on the horn. "I'm not wanted by the law, if that's what you're asking."

"You're trespassin'!" the young man accused.

"I'm doing a favor for a dead man," Tanner insisted quietly.

"I think we ought to search the bastard," replied the young man. "What do you think, Quince?"

The rifleman shook his head. "We'll take him in an' let your pa size him up. Give up your gun, mister."

"You men are making a big mistake," said Tanner. "You got no call to be doing it like this."

"Shut up," ordered the kid. "Unbutton that coat and hand over your six-gun, easy."

Tanner obeyed, and the same moment the third man moved in from behind and snatched Tanner's Winchester from its scabbard.

"Move out," ordered the one called Quince. "Billy, you bring up drag. If he tries to make a run for it, wing 'im. Brace, you bring in the old man's body."

As the horses moved forward, Tanner felt flakes of wet snow strike him in the face. By the time they reached the lights of the ranch house, huge, wet snowflakes clung to their shoulders, hats, and horses' manes.

A lighted veranda shouldered the large, two-story house, and light streamed from the ground-floor windows. The house radiated warmth out into the swirling snow. Tanner could make out figures moving about inside.

"Wait here," ordered Quince, swinging from the saddle. "I'll get the boss. Watch him, Billy." His boots creaked in the new snow as he tied off his horse to the rail and climbed the steps to the veranda.

In response to Quince's knock, the door opened and the form of a woman was outlined against the kerosene lights. Tanner could not make out what was said, but after a moment the door closed and Quince, hands thrust deep in the pockets of his greatcoat, paced restlessly on the porch.

A full five minutes passed before the door was again opened, this time revealing the silhouette of a short, heavy, round-shouldered man. He appeared to listen to Quince for a moment, and shook his head emphatically. He gave a few brief instructions and then turned back into the house, closing the door sharply in Quince's face.

Quince slogged down the steps to the horses and said to the young man, "Yer pa wants Tanner inside, Billy. You take care of the horses. Brace, take the old man's body down to the icehouse. Get one of the boys to give you a hand." He added soberly, "An' you boys give Tanner back his guns."

Brace rode alongside the Appaloosa and shoved Tanner's rifle back into the scabbard.

Billy opened his mouth to protest, but Quince waved him silent. "Boss's orders. Give 'im his six-gun." He turned to Tanner and said, "Step down an' come inside. Mr. Tate would like to talk to you."

Tanner stepped down, passed the Appaloosa's reins to the scowling young man, and accepted the six-gun thrust sullenly at him.

"Don't grain Jake too heavy, boy," he instructed Billy. He turned toward the house and then threw back at the angry young man, "Give the old man's mare a good feed. She's earned it."

He followed Quince up the steps, aware of Billy's glaring fury on his back.

CHAPTER 2

"FIRST, I'd like to express my gratitude, Mr. Tanner, for bringing Rooster in. We've been searching for him for two days, but the snow up in that country really hampered us. He rode for me for thirty years. More a member of the family than a hand."

John Tate was a gnomelike man with shoulders rolled forward and a hump protruding from the upper middle of his back. He stood by the fireplace with his arm resting on the mantle at what appeared to be, because of his shortness, a most uncomfortable angle.

"And secondly, I need to apologize for the way my men roughed you up. My son Billy's headstrong, but Quince should've known better."

"No harm done." Tanner sipped at the fine bourbon in his hand and basked in the comforting warmth of the fireplace. He stretched his long legs out before him, sunk a bit deeper into the leather chair, and let his tired gaze wander about the richly furnished room.

"I do feel I owe you something, Mr. Tanner. If you would not consider it in bad taste, I'd like to give you a reward. Say, a hundred dollars?"

"One hundred dollars!" Tanner answered, aghast. "That's far too generous, Mr. Tate, and it isn't necessary. Under the circumstances, anyone would've done the same thing. I would appreciate a place to sleep for the night. And I'll need to get my bedroll. It's wrapped around the old man."

"You won't be needing your bedroll tonight. You'll stay right here in the house. We've three guest rooms."

Tate moved to a walnut library table and took out two

cigars. "These come special from New Orleans," he said, passing one to Tanner.

They went through the ritual of lighting up, after which Tate seated himself opposite Tanner and in like manner stretched his stubby legs in the direction of the fire.

"We don't find too many men brave enough to try crossing the Cut Throat in the dead of winter. Must've been something very important to start you on your way."

Tanner smiled through the cigar smoke. "You have a more delicate way of asking than your son, but the question's the same. No, Mr. Tate, I'm not on the run. Never been in trouble or wanted by the law in my life."

"Didn't mean to pry," Tate replied, grinning. "But you've got to admit you're a bit of an oddity."

"I'm forty-four years old," Tanner answered slowly. "I don't have a lot of time to waste. There's things I still want to do with my life."

Tate nodded. "I admire ambition. Without trying to pry, Mr. Tanner, just what kind of plans have you got lined up for yourself?"

Tanner smiled to himself: relentless little bastard.

"It's no secret, Mr. Tate, that I plan to get me a little horse operation going, first thing come spring."

"That's good. Good." Tate beamed, maybe a bit too enthusiastically to suit Tanner. "Of course, even if you were to venture it in a small way, it's going to take a little capital."

"A little's what I got. I'm hoping it'll be enough to get me started. From then on, who knows?"

"Excellent. Well, if you get in a tight, I might still be of help to you. Besides the ranch here, I run the bank in Sweetwater. Our business is making loans to responsible, hardworking ranchers."

Tate hesitated. "Uh, did Rooster have much to say before he passed on? As I say, he was nearly family."

Tanner felt his eyes growing heavy from fatigue and bourbon. "Not much. He just didn't want to be left in that cabin over the winter." Something floated in the back of his mind, something else he had considered telling this man . . . about the dead horse . . . but it could wait until the morning.

Tate rose to his feet. "You look done in, my friend. I took the liberty of having a bath drawn for you."

He walked to the door, which, from the sounds issuing from beyond, could only be the kitchen.

"Charlotte," he called.

A moment later a small, elderly black woman appeared. She squinted at Tanner through a pair of round wire-rimmed spectacles.

"Charlotte, is Mr. Tanner's water ready?" Tate turned to Tanner. "When you've finished, Charlotte will have some hot food for you. After that, I'm sure you'll be ready to retire."

Tanner nodded gratefully and nearly staggered when he rose to his feet.

After the bath, Tanner ate a lonely but satisfying meal of fried chicken at a table in the kitchen. When he had finished, Charlotte showed him upstairs to a bedroom.

The room was furnished as one in an expensive hotel: a chair, a small divan, mahogany table with an exquisite stained-glass lamp aglow. There was a thick carpet on the floor, and near the wall, a massive four-poster with a down comforter turned back to expose crisp, white sheets.

Tanner sat on the bed in a stupor, arms and legs leaden, head throbbing. Exhausted as he was, he considered the fact that he should tell someone—perhaps the law, if not Tate himself—about the horse. It had to mean something. . . .

Tanner nearly dozed off sitting on the edge of the bed.

He roused himself enough to pull his boots off and lay his six-gun on the bedside stand. One last bleary afterthought prompted him to cross the room to the closed door and wedge a straight-back chair under the handle. Within moments, he was asleep.

CHAPTER 3

AT twenty-six, Eleanor Tate's skin maintained the elastic smoothness of youth and her chiseled features carried the softness and sensuousness of vulnerability. Her blond hair, rich and full, hung to her shoulders in gentle waves, being tossed and tumbled like the mane of a wild young filly.

Altogether, she was thoroughly captivating to Lee Tanner as he collided with her in the hall in the morning. He had closed the bedroom door, turned, and bumped into her with such force as to make her take a quick step back, hand to her throat, eyes wide.

"Forgive me, ma'am," he finally stammered. "I surely didn't see you."

Eleanor stood silent, distrustful, aloof.

"Hope I didn't hurt you," he said apologetically.

"I've been bumped by my horse much harder," she said without enthusiasm. She seemed to consider him a moment. "I need some coffee," she said. "I think we could both use some."

Tanner knew how he must appear to her. He had a three-day crop of whiskers, sunken cheeks, and a gash on his forehead, inflicted when he had raked himself passing under a pine snag. Altogether, not much to dazzle a young lady. Couple that with the smell of campfires and stale sweat on his clothes . . . He winced.

In a matter-of-fact tone, she said, "My name is Eleanor Tate. I trust you're a friend of Daddy's?"

"Not exactly," he answered, a bit embarrassed. He felt awkward. "What . . . I mean to say," he said, faltering, "I found an old man up in the mountains and brought him down. Your daddy . . . father was kind enough to let me stay over."

"You're the one who brought Rooster in?"

"Yes. By the way, before he passed on, the old gent said to tell Eleanor something. All things accounted for, you must be the Eleanor he meant."

She looked guarded.

"He said to tell Eleanor it's all over. She can rest now. Does that mean anything?"

She reflected for a moment, wrinkling her brow. At last she shook her head. "Doesn't make any sense to me. Poor old dear must have been delirious."

He nodded. "That occurred to me too."

"Rooster practically raised me," she said, a trace of wistfulness breaking through. "Taught me horses and riding, roping, practically everything. Daddy was always so busy in town."

"It's hard to picture you on a horse," he observed as they started down the oak staircase. "Much less slinging a rope."

"You think that sort of thing's beneath a lady?" she asked, pausing on the stairs.

"I don't think it's beneath anyone. Hard work never is. By the same token, I hate to see a racehorse pull a plow."

She smiled. "I'll take your comparing me to a horse as a compliment." She continued down the stairs and led him through a doorway into an elegant dining room. At one end of the long table sat John Tate, busily attacking a mound of pancakes. He looked up as the couple entered and grinned.

"Eleanor. Good morning, my dear. And you, Mr. Tanner. I see you've met my daughter."

"It's been my pleasure," Tanner answered, holding the chair for the woman and then seating himself beside her.

Tate stopped chewing and scrutinized his silent daughter. "Honey, I'm just real sorry about old Rooster."

"Daddy, it's just terrible. Poor, dear old man." She bowed her head, fingering the edge of the tablecloth.

"It's a real pity, all right. Had Mr. Tanner not happened along, he might well have died all alone." Tate wiped his lips on a snowy napkin. "I'd like to say again, Mr. Tanner, we're grateful."

Tanner smiled but said nothing. He may have appeared modest, but the truth was he had never in all his life felt as dirty and smelly as at this moment. In the space of a few short minutes with this beautiful lady, he had suddenly become concerned about his appearance. He must, he vowed, get to town and do something about it.

"Mr. Tanner is planning on starting a horse ranch, dear," said Tate. "I've been thinking about the old Whiteman place, over by the 'Dobes. There's plenty good grass, and not much higher country than right around here. And I think, besides the graze, Whiteman had about twenty acres or so of oats, as I recall. At least that much ground would be broke to the plow."

"That spot could make a lovely ranch," Eleanor agreed. "If it were cleaned up and taken care of. When I was little, Rooster would take me riding in the foothills above there. There's an old clay bank back in a box canyon where he taught me to shoot." She placed a quick hand to her mouth and shook her head, eyes closed. "Oh dear," she whispered.

Tanner felt drawn toward her, finding her even more alluring by this sudden show of vulnerability.

"Well," Tate observed with an encouraging smile. "Lose one old friend, gain a new one."

"Have you a first name, Mr. Tanner?" Eleanor asked suddenly.

"It's Lee. And I would be real pleased to be on a first-name basis with you folks." He looked a bit too long into her eyes until she smiled a bit coquettishly.

"You're welcome in our home anytime, Lee," said Tate. He pushed away from the table and rose. "Well, I must be on my way," he announced. He kissed Eleanor's forehead and gave

Tanner a fatherly pat on the shoulder before heading out of the room.

"Eleanor," Tate said, pausing in the doorway, "if you have the time, perhaps you could show Lee the Whiteman place. Just a suggestion." He waved cheerily and was gone.

Her gaze turned to Tanner slowly. "I have plans for today, but I can be free tomorrow afternoon," she said.

Tanner wished she had sounded more enthusiastic. "I'd like that very much," he said. "And tomorrow would be good for me, too. I've got to get settled in town today." Tanner smiled and dug into his stack of pancakes. He felt good. He felt pretty damn good.

The first stop for Tanner was Tate's bank. There he deposited most of the cash in his money belt. Next, he tied the Appaloosa to the rack before Tate's Mercantile and spent the next half hour buying clothes. He purchased several pairs of new Levi's jeans, shirts, and underwear, and a box of cartridges for his rifle. On his way to the hotel, he had spotted a barbershop, and, after checking into a room, he headed back that way, new clothes under his arm.

After his shave and haircut, Tanner treated himself to the use of the bathing facilities in the back room. It was unusual to bathe two days in a row, but he had over a week's worth of trail dust, so one washing only teased the dirt. Besides, Eleanor Tate was worth this much, and more. He settled in the hot water and lazily watched the Chinese attendant fill the tub in the next stall.

As he relaxed in the tub, he endeavored to get a handle on the events of the past two days. Instead of limping into town and scratching around for a toehold as he had expected, he had fallen into a situation that showed real promise. In their conversation at breakfast, Eleanor had confided to him that her father had only recently foreclosed on the Whiteman place. The bank was anxious to sell, and she was sure, should Tanner decide he wanted the property, that her father would use his considerable influence to overcome any problems that might stand in the way.

Tanner's thoughts turned to Eleanor, and he smiled in a self-satisfied way. He hoped he was not reading too much into her behavior toward him.

As Tanner soaked, a lanky cowhand entered the bathroom and began taking off his clothes, tossing each item carelessly upon the wall pegs.

It was only as the man was stepping gingerly into the hot tub next to Tanner's that their eyes happened to meet.

"Well, fer God's sake!" exclaimed the man. "If it ain't old Lee Tanner!"

Tanner looked closely into the pale gray eyes. "Troy? Troy Sams? Well, I'll be go-to-hell." He reached a wet hand across to clasp the one offered. "Where in hell did you drop from?"

"That'll be my question, you ornery ol' sumbitch. Last I heard, you was still in Colorado, ranchin' with yer folks. What brings you out this way?"

"Needed a change of scenery, I guess. Hope to get me an operation going out here somewhere."

Sams settled down into the hot water with gasps, groans, and pleasurable sighs. He ducked his head under the steaming water and came up sputtering, blond hair plastered to his skull. His large ears, hidden before by the mop of hair, stuck out like jug handles. He wiped the water from his eyes and settled back into the tub until, like Tanner, only his head was visible above the top of the tub.

"Well, let me tell you, Lee," he said amiably, "this is a good area, but it's pretty well sewed up." He wrinkled his forehead and stared up at the ceiling. "You got yer McIntoshes, yer Blakes, both big and greedy. Nice folks, but both hell-rippers. And then, of course, there's Tate. Between the three of them, they pretty much run things. There's really no such thing as open range with them three."

"It's a big valley," Tanner said. "They can't claim it all."

"Oh, there's a few smaller ones, all right." Sams pulled one huge foot from the water and propped it on the tub rim. "Jess Grant's one. I been workin' fer him. Lee Tully, down by the 'Dobes—few miles south of the Whiteman place. There's Andy Farley and his daughter. But them outfits are small potatoes. Just hanging on. Not much room fer any new customers."

Sams lathered himself with the thick soap, rubbing it into his hair, squinting against the sting. Then he faced Tanner and proclaimed, "I got me a *in*." He submerged himself to rinse off the soap. When he came up, he said, "I'm going to marry me that Farley girl and then me an' her daddy are goin' to be partners." He laughed, got out of the tub, and began toweling himself. "Now, pull yer lazy carcass out of there—I'm buyin' you a drink or six."

Tanner could see that Troy Sams had not changed. He was enjoyable to be around, always quick with a joke, but also capable of unusual subtlety. Tanner recalled that the young man had had many friends. About eight years back, the two had worked a summer breaking mounts for the army, and Tanner had grown to like the rowdy young man and his boisterous acceptance of life.

There was a saloon on either side of the barbershop, and they chose the one to the right. At a quiet table near the back, they exchanged the news of the last eight years.

"Let me tell you about this Farley gal," Sams said excitedly, as though bragging on a new six-gun. "She's real purty, but not too purty, if you know what I mean."

"You're really going to marry this one? Seems to me I recall you've had more than your share of pretty girls."

Sams nodded enthusiastically. "I'm tellin' ya, she's just right fer me, Lee. Quiet, where I'm loud. You know me—I like raisin' a little hell once in a while. I'll put some spice in her life, an' she'll put a little peace an' calm in mine. But now, that's not to say she don't like to josh a fella and kid around herself once in a while. And her ol' man's all right, too. A real hardworkin' bastard. If any of these little ranchers stand a chance of makin' it, it'll be Farley."

"What about the Whiteman place?" Tanner broke in. "What can you tell me?"

"It ain't a bad spread," Sams answered disinterestedly. "Ol' Man Whiteman kind of let it go to hell. Just lost interest, I guess. Got lazy. Finally, he just let the bank have it. Why do you ask?"

"I'm supposed to ride out and have a look at it tomorrow. Eleanor Tate's going to show me around."

Troy Sams's jaw dropped. "Eleanor Tate? How did you ever meet up with her?"

Something crackled in the air. Tanner paused, then answered evenly, "I did a favor for her father."

Sams appeared embarrassed. "Oh. Well . . ." He floundered. "Say," he said, suddenly jovial again, holding up his empty glass. "Your arm broke, is it?"

Tanner picked up the bottle and poured whiskey into both glasses. They drank, and Tanner began to share his plans with Sams.

"I want to put together a brood mare band, maybe fifteen or twenty head. And then maybe get a contract over at Fort Grover to supply them with mounts. I figure to go around scouting out the grade horses for that, to begin with. Just me to do the breaking. I think I can make out all right just off the Army."

"You're going to need a good stud to go along with them mares," Sams said, "an' I just happen to know where one hangs out, along with a couple of fine mares. Interested?"

"I wouldn't be buying anything until I get a place," Tanner said. "But it sure wouldn't do no harm to look."

"Let's go." Sams pushed his chair back with a loud scrape. When they reached the street, he said, "Besides the stud and the mares, there's a little filly I want to get your opinion on. Looks to be pretty fine breedin' stock herself one day."

"Out of what line?" Tanner asked innocently.

"She's out of the Farley line," Sams answered with a wink. "Miss Carrie Lynn Farley herself."

CHAPTER 4

IT was an hour's ride in a brisk winter's head wind to the Farley place. Tanner felt frozen to the saddle when he and Sams topped out the ridge overlooking the neat ranch house and outbuildings.

Tanner took in the layout with an appreciative eye: neat grounds around the stock pens, a new-looking hay barn, a few small sheds for hay equipment. Someone had done considerable planning and work.

Fifty or sixty head of whiteface cows and calves milled about in the sturdy pens, bawling angrily as a haywagon pulled up. A slight figure crawled into the back and began pitching hay into the feed bunkers next to the fence.

Tanner nudged the Appaloosa with his knees and started down the slope in the wake of Sams bay gelding.

The figure pitching hay paused at the approach of the two riders, stood the pitchfork up against the back of the wagon seat, and casually picked up a rifle.

"Don't shoot, little darlin'," called Sams, and he pulled the bay to a walk. "I ain't come to carry you off just yet."

"You crazy fool!" she scolded. "I told you always to holler out before you come ridin' in. You'll get your scalp parted down the middle with a bullet one of these days."

Tanner halted beside Sams at the wagon, and he saw a slightly boyish-looking face peer from under the folds of a wool cap. A fleece-lined coat was buttoned up to the chin. The girl laid the rifle on the wagon seat and, with a small gloved hand, took a perfunctory swipe at her small red nose.

"Jess give you an extra day off, or did he get smart and

21

fire you?" she inquired, pulling off the wool cap to reveal short, curly brown hair.

"I tol' the boss I had me a beautiful young lady to propose to. But she turned me down, so I thought I'd come out and torment you instead."

"Sounds like she's got a whale lot more sense than I got," the girl quipped back. "Course, when you're homely as me, you're used to takin' someone else's leftovers."

"You ain't that homely," Sams defended stoutly. "Not once a fella gets off a ways. Kinda like a rocky hillside looks all smooth an' nice from the next hill over."

She threw her wool hat at his face. "I *would* have to fish for a compliment. Who's your quiet friend on the pretty spotted horse?"

"Carrie, this gent is Lee Tanner, busted-down old hoss wrangler from Colorado. He'll be our best man when an' if I take pity an' marry you."

Tanner touched the brim of his hat. "I'm pleased to meet you, ma'am."

"I got to say one thing, Tanner," she said, "you ain't particular of the company you keep."

Her smile was warm and friendly, and Tanner wondered how the round of jokes concerning her homeliness had gotten their start. She appeared to be in her early twenties, and not only was she not unattractive, she was actually quite pretty, even though her full lips were chapped and her cheeks were windburned. She had that softly burning glow that indicated health and vitality. Troy Sams was right: she would be a good partner for a hardworking rancher.

"Dad's in the house," she said, picking up the pitchfork. "His turn to fix supper. You two ride on up an' have some coffee, while I finish the chores." She resumed filling the feed bunkers, forking the hay from the wagon in long, powerful strokes.

"Don't forget to muck them stalls out 'fore you come up," Sams called over his shoulder with a quick grin at Tanner.

As they approached the house, a smallish, muscular man in shirt-sleeves walked out onto the porch. A six-gun was strapped to his waist, and he scanned Tanner with a friendly but cautious eye.

"I knew it was you right off, Troy, when I heard Carrie yell. Don't believe I recognize this gent, though."

"Mr. Farley, shake hands with Lee Tanner, friend of mine from down the road a bit."

Tanner dismounted and clasped the outstretched hand.

"You got a real nice place here, Mr. Farley," Tanner said.

"Took a while, but we're gettin' there. Me and Mrs. Farley settled in here about twenty years ago. Carrie was two, as I recall." He slapped his bare arms. "Come on inside before I freeze to death. Coffee's hot, and supper'll be ready soon."

Farley led the way through a neat front room with sturdy, handmade furniture into a warm and beckoning kitchen. He motioned the two men to straight-back chairs. Tanner and Sams stripped off their coats and hung them on the backs of the chairs, while Farley poured coffee for the three of them. The room was very hot from the wood range, and the smell of frying chicken and potatoes was well-nigh overwhelming.

Tanner found the coffee delicious. He settled back against the chair and stretched his long legs under the table.

"I brought Lee out to show him those mares of yours," Sams said. "Lee's goin' to be puttin' together a horse operation soon's he can get situated."

Farley eyed Tanner speculatively. "You a horseman, Tanner?"

"He ain't never done nothin' else," Sams volunteered. "Best damn bronc fighter you ever seen!"

Boots stomped on the porch outside the kitchen door, and shortly afterward Carrie Farley brushed into the room, accompanied by a blast of cold air and a flutter of flakes.

"Spittin' snow again," she commented needlessly, pulling off her stocking cap and gloves. She moved over to the cook stove and held her hands close, rubbing warmth into them.

She turned around abruptly and, ignoring Sams and Tanner, said, "Dad, I don't like the way Carl's treating that stallion. He's going to make him mean."

Farley pushed himself away from the table. "Sit down and rest a bit, little gal. Have some coffee." He walked to the stove and poured a cup, while the girl shrugged out of her coat and dropped wearily to a chair.

"You didn't go messin' with Carl again, did you?" her father asked. "Stallion's got to know who's boss."

"He's too damn rough with him!" she blurted out. "Downright cruel. He's got him in the bitting rig, cinched up tight enough to break his jaw. And he ain't working him either, Dad. He's planning on leaving him in the rig overnight!"

"You don't say so." Farley's cup stopped midway to his lips. "You must be mistaken, honey."

"No, I ain't neither. Carl's down at the bunkhouse, sprucin' up to go into town."

"That don't sound right to me," commented Sams with far more seriousness in his tone than was usual.

There were a few moments of silence, and then Farley turned to Tanner. "What's your opinion?"

He hesitated a moment. "Each man works a horse a bit different. I wouldn't want any man telling me how to break a horse without my asking him."

"Well, it's my horse, and I'm asking."

Tanner stared into his cup. Could be the man's treatment of the horse looked worse than it actually was, he was thinking. When you're training a horse, lots of things appear cruel that don't actually hurt the animal. Horses, and most large beasts, have a high tolerance for pain. But if the trainer was doing his job right, he should never have to overuse pain as a tool of discipline.

"Guess it wouldn't do no harm to have a look," Tanner said reluctantly.

Two men lounged around the wood stove in the small frame bunkhouse. A third stood over the washbasin, combing his hair in a ragged shard of broken mirror. Everyone's eyes turned to the door as Carrie entered, followed by her father, Troy Sams, and a stranger.

"Gentry, we've come to have a look at the stud," said Farley. "Where you got him?"

The one who had been combing his hair looked puzzled, sizing up Tanner with a speculative glance.

"In the small pen behind the barn. Why?" The *why* was as near to insolence as one could come without going over the line. Gentry was a big man, broad and handsome, with narrow hips and long powerful arms. His gaze drifted over to Carrie, who held a lantern.

"You been tellin' tales out of school, Carrie?" he asked with an easy, relaxed smile, flashing dazzling white teeth beneath a dark mustache.

"I've told Dad just what I seen." Her eyes glinted. "You've been mistreating that horse."

Gentry ignored the accusation and stared at Tanner. "I don't believe I know this gent," he said. "You hire you another man, Mr. Farley?"

"We're talking horses now," answered Farley, moving to the door. "Come on down to the pen. I want a look at that horse." He took the lantern from Carrie and led the way to a pole corral behind the barn.

It was snowing heavily now, and the large wet flakes quickly covered hats and shoulders. With the barn downwind, there was no cover in the pen.

The stallion stood on the side of the pen closest to the barn, very still in the shadows, as though hiding from the lantern light.

Farley handed the lantern to Carrie. "Carrie, crawl up on that fence and hold the light high."

Tanner slipped between the poles into the corral. Farley

and Troy followed while Gentry remained outside, resting his arms on the top rail next to where Carrie sat with the lantern.

He was a small horse, Tanner reckoned, standing maybe fifteen hands at best, a thousand pounds even.

The animal stood with its head almost perpendicular to the ground, held in that position by a leather rein on either side, running from the bit shanks to rings in a leather strap behind its withers. The horse was trembling, and the whites of its large eyes loomed in the lantern glow. A black smear clung to the lower lip and gathered at the corner of the mouth. The animal's distress was apparent.

"What the hell kind of bit you got on him?" Tanner demanded. He grabbed the bridle on the near side and jerked free the slipknot holding the rein to the shoulder ring. Still hanging on to the bridle, he moved the horse around and freed the rein on the off side.

"I always start my horses on a twisted wire snaffle. Then if they show rank, like this one, I put 'em on a spade," Gentry answered, a knife edge to his voice. "I don't feel I have to explain a damn thing to you, mister."

"You're explaining it to *me*, Gentry," interjected Farley.

Tanner crossed the reins and knotted them above the horse's neck. He unbuckled the throat strap, pulled the bridle forward over the horse's ears, and let the heavy bit drop from the stallion's mouth into his left hand.

The stallion shook his head and mane, and flecks of blood and foam spattered against Tanner's cheek.

"Mr. Farley," Gentry said, raising his voice, "part of my job when you hired me was to break out the new stock. I do the best job, and I do it as fast as I can. I been doing it like that for years, and nobody's ever complained before!"

"Maybe nobody ever asked the hosses before," offered Sams with a baiting grin.

Tanner unhooked the heavy bit from the headstall and silently handed it to Farley.

Farley examined the blood-stained instrument. On the

crossbar between the two shanks, where a conventional bit would impose only a smooth loop of steel on the horse's mouth, there was welded instead a triangular, spoon-shaped bit of metal, approximately two inches long. The severity of the bit was immediately apparent to Farley. The extra length of the spade would double the leverage and the pressure placed on the animal's jawbone. Additionally, the smooth edges of the spade would unhesitatingly cut through a horse's tongue; a sharp yank on the reins in the hands of an inexperienced or cruel rider could do irreparable damage to the horse's mouth. Any horse trussed up in the bitting rig with one of these, with no relief from the pressure, would endure unrelenting agony.

Holding onto the reins around the stallion's neck, Tanner gently rubbed the animal's sweating shoulder and spoke soothingly into the twitching ears. After a moment, the horse responded, rubbing its muzzle on Tanner's sleeve.

"Will you look at that!" exclaimed Sams. "There's your rank stud, Gentry. Just like a damn puppy dawg."

"What about the horse, Tanner?" Farley asked evenly.

Tanner's jaws were clinched tightly. There was cruelty of all kinds in the West, and he had seen his share. But a helpless animal subjected to needless pain was something he had never been able to accept.

He slipped the looped reins up just behind the ears, took a half-turn around the muzzle to fashion a halter. "Get him into a stall. Rub him down. Give him some grain. Show him he can expect to be treated decently by some folks." He looked directly into Gentry's eyes.

Carrie dropped from her perch on the fence and pulled open the corral gate.

"There's stalls in the hay barn," she said. Slogging in the lead through the mud and slush, she helped Tanner usher the prancing, nervous stallion into a stall within the snug barn.

Farley, Sams, and the fuming Gentry remained behind at

the corral. Tanner could hear the sharp exchange as he rubbed the horse down with some old burlap he found in the stall.

Carrie produced a bucket of oats and held the bucket while the horse munched the grain.

"Do you think Carl's ruined the horse?" she asked, watching him rub down the animal's filthy legs.

He straightened up slowly, stiffly, and rested his arm across the horse's withers. "No. I don't think so. Depends on what comes next. I sure don't recommend turning him back over to that idiot."

It was warm and cozy in the stall. Fresh straw covered the floor. The horse munched contentedly on the grain, and the barn was filled with the smell of wet horse, pungent manure, and the sweet scent of cured alfalfa.

"Gentry's all we got," Carrie said. "You know how hard it is on the horses in the spring and fall. We work 'em till they drop. Each hand goes through a half-dozen saddle changes a day. We get new horses each year that need breakin' and none of the other hands want to fool with it."

Tanner slapped the horse on the shoulder and stepped from the stall, followed by Carrie. He latched the door behind her.

"Anyone can train a horse," he said. "Just takes time. And patience. My advice is get rid of them mares and the young stuff. Keep just what you need and concentrate on that."

"Do you think I could learn to do it?" she asked, eyes glowing with sudden excitement. "I know nothing about breaking horses, but I can ride. And I know what I want a horse to be able to do."

Tanner was amused but at the same time impressed, this slip of a girl talking about breaking a horse. And yet, he reasoned, why not? After all, it wasn't a question of strength. Even the strongest man would come out on the short end matching strength with a horse. You had to use your brains.

And it was plain this girl, despite her lack of book learning, had intelligence.

He answered slowly, "I've seen some mean stallions do some pretty ugly things. I heard tell of a rank stud one time got a man down and ripped off his arm."

Carrie's eyes went wide, deep pools in the yellow lamp glow. Tanner noticed again how attractive she was, damp hair curled about her oval face, lips pursed in a concentrated grimace. Troy was a lucky man to be joining up with such a mighty fine woman. Troy had smartened up considerably since the old days.

"Stallions can go crazy and destroy everything around them," he continued, "or they can calmly reach through the fence and bite the spine of a foal in two, right from under the mare."

The stories weren't exaggerated, and he wasn't trying to frighten her. He just didn't want her going into something on his say-so that might get her hurt. At least not without knowing some of the facts.

"They're not all that way," she said defensively. "He's not." They watched the stallion calmly search out the last particle of grain from the bottom of the bucket.

The arguing voices outside had faded into the soft moan of the storm.

"We best be getting back," Tanner said, taking the lantern from her. "Sounds like they've taken the battle back to the house."

She was hesitant, grasping his arm. "Well, do you think I could? Tell me." Her eyes searched his eagerly.

"I got to be honest with you," he answered after a moment. "You might get your head kicked in if you're not real careful. In case you haven't noticed, that horse outweighs you a mite. And,"—he paused significantly—"there's some tricks a person needs to know to make the job easier."

"You could show me, couldn't you? Just a little, to get me started?"

Tanner shook his head. He just wouldn't have the time.

"I'm busy scouting me out a place of my own," he said. "If at all possible, I want to be situated and operating by spring."

"This is only December. Surely you can spare a little time. How about tomorrow?" she insisted with an impish smile.

Tanner was about to decline when he realized tomorrow morning he would be free. Eleanor was to take him out to the Whiteman place in the afternoon.

"All right," he said, giving in with a helpless grin. "We'll try it in the morning for a while."

As he and the girl worked their way through the snow back to the house, Tanner glanced up at the black sky and the heavily swirling flakes. He remarked to Carrie, "Troy and I better be going soon, before it's too late."

CHAPTER 5

BECAUSE of the storm, Tanner and Sams had spent the night wrapped in blankets on the Farley's front-room floor. When Tanner awoke at first light, his heart sank. The snow the storm had deposited overnight made it doubtful that he and Eleanor Tate would be taking any pleasure rides today.

He moved about in his stocking feet, stoking up the fire in the wood heater and rolling up his bed. Taking care to make as little noise as possible, he pulled on his boots and coat and slipped outside.

Despite the snow, the air was almost mild. Or so it felt to Tanner. Chinook brewing, he thought hopefully, breaking his way through to the barn.

For a half hour, Tanner looked to the feeding of the horses in the barn and those in the pen outside, and then slogged his way back to the house.

When he stepped onto the porch, he smelled the aroma of coffee brewing and heard voices in the kitchen.

Inside, he found Farley and Sams seated at the table, Sams in his sock feet. Carrie was laying strips of bacon into a pan on the stove, a curling wisp of hair clinging to her forehead.

"Good news," Tanner announced, slipping off his coat and settling into a chair at the table. "Chinook on the way. Few hours there won't be enough snow left to make a decent-size snowball."

Farley poured coffee for Tanner and refilled his own and Sams's cups.

"That'll be welcome," Farley commented, resuming his seat at the table. "Snow's fine except when you got stock out in it you have to care for. We got a hundred and sixty head we'll be hauling hay to this morning."

"Me an' Tanner'll give you a hand," said Sams. "I don't have to be back to work 'til tomorrow."

Tanner held his breath. He didn't have time to get involved in a long feeding chore.

"Thanks," said Farley, "but no need. Parsons and Rawlins can handle it. Right now I got more help than I need anyhow. About all they can do is feed and fix fence."

Tanner tasted the coffee and found it hot and good.

After breakfast over more coffee, the conversation turned to the matter that had brought Tanner out to the ranch to begin with.

"Did you happen to look over those mares this morning?" asked Farley.

"If I was looking at the right ones, they'll do just fine. Provided we can get together on a price. And you'll have to hold them for me until I can get set up with a place."

Farley stretched back in his chair and looked at Tanner sagely. "You know, those are probably the best breeding stock you're going to find around these parts."

Tanner caught Carrie trying to suppress a grin. "Dad's a born horse trader, Lee. Watch out."

"An' Lee knows horseflesh," offered Sams. "We might have us a Mexican standoff in the works."

"Oh, by the way, Dad," said Carrie. "I noticed Carl's horse was gone when Lee and I walked past the bunkhouse last night. What happened between you two, anyway?"

"I fired the son of a bitch, that's what."

"Great!" exclaimed Carrie. "From now on, I'll do the breaking." She cast a mischievous glance at Tanner. "Lee already said he'd help me. And we'll start with the stud, first thing this morning."

For an hour Tanner worked the young stallion, while the girl watched. He and Carrie had brought the horse from the barn into the round pole corral, where Tanner rigged a twenty-foot lead line to the halter and began walking the horse in large circles around the perimeter of the pen. After a time, he had the horse moving out on its own on the end of the line, while Tanner stood in the center like an axle.

When the horse would walk steadily, first to the left and then to the right, Tanner pushed it up into a trot and from there into a lope. Holding the lead line in his left hand, he whistled and beat his hat on his thigh to urge the horse to move out at the quickened pace.

When man and horse had worked the snow in the corral into a sea of muddy slush, Tanner brought the animal to a halt with a sharp "Whoa!" and a tug on the line. Coiling the line as he went, he moved up to the animal. He stroked the horse's sweating neck and spoke in soft tones of praise.

From her perch on the fence rail, Carrie felt a lump well up in her throat. The man's love of horses was as clear to her as it must have been to the stallion. The horse stood still, ears up, eyes bright and eager and unafraid.

Tanner gave the horse one final slap on the shoulder and led it over to the fence.

"That's enough for now," he said to Carrie. "Walk him, cool him down. Give him a good grooming, and then put him away." He smiled up at her. "Do this every day. In a while you should be able to ease a saddle up on his back. Take it real slow all the way. Make sure he understands one thing before you try to push him into something new."

She dropped lightly from the fence and took the lead rope from him.

"I'll cool him down," she said eagerly. "You go on up to the house and have some coffee." She smiled at him. "I take this to mean that you might drop around now and then and work with me on this beast?"

"I'm going to be busy, but I'll do what I can," Lee promised. He had to fight to suppress his own grin, wondering if maybe she had worked him the way he had just worked the colt.

He slipped through the pole fence and slogged through the melting snow to the house.

The main street of Sweetwater was a sea of mud. Wagons churned through the ooze, animals strained, men cursed, and women negotiated to the boardwalks with their skirts held high.

It was early afternoon, and Tanner was anxious to clean up and get himself out to the Tate ranch. His heart raced with excitement at the thought of seeing Eleanor Tate again. He hoped she would not be put off by the weather. It was, after all, continuing to warm up, and the sky was clearing off nicely.

Tanner and Sams said good-bye at the hotel. "Kind of rushed, Troy. I'll be seein' you later."

Sams grinned knowingly, waved, and passed on.

In his room, Tanner shed his muddy Levi's for a second new pair, shaved, and put on a fresh shirt. He knotted a clean bandanna around his neck and was trying to brush new life into his old hat when a knock sounded at the door.

"Sheriff Reynolds, Tanner. I'd like a word with you."

Tanner opened the door to a buffalo-sized man in a leather jacket with a fur collar, over a great sloping mass of shoulders. Bright red suspenders, seen through the open jacket front, supported a preposterous stomach hanging several inches over his pants. Sheriff Reynolds's appearance would have been comic but for the cold, businesslike gleam in his dark eyes. An amber walrus mustache was draped across his upper lip, and his cheek rolled with a massive cud of tobacco.

A Colt, suspended from a full cartridge belt, hung so low on his hip it threatened to drag down his pants. The walnut grip of the weapon, Tanner noted, was worn smooth.

"Sheriff, come on in," invited Tanner. "I'm sorry I don't

have time for a long visit. I have another appointment this afternoon."

"This won't take long," the sheriff answered past the tobacco roll. "Tate told about your good deed for Rooster Barstow, and I just wanted to clear up a couple of things."

"Shoot." Lee took a seat on the edge of the bed.

The sheriff glanced about the room, taking in each detail, appraising Tanner with a practiced eye. "I would like to know a little more about yourself, Mr. Tanner." His searching eyes locked on Tanner's.

"Whatever you want to know, Sheriff." Tanner returned the sheriff's gaze steadily.

Reynolds nodded thoughtfully, strolled across the room, and paused before the window. With one finger he pulled aside the lace curtain, and he casually scanned the busy main street below. He turned lazily and leaned his disproportionately small buttocks against the sill post.

"Understand you're from Colorado. Leave anything behind I might need to know about?" he asked mildly.

"The sheriff in Ouray knows me," Tanner answered. "If you want to know about my character, he'll vouch for me. Send him a telegram. His name's Roy Patton."

Reynolds eyed Tanner in silence a moment. "I might do that. Right now I'm askin' you."

The lawman's manner was beginning to nettle Tanner. "I was what you might call an upstanding citizen. You want to know anything else, you'll have to find out for yourself. Now, what's all this about? I can't rightly believe that you slap every newcomer to the valley up against the wall and throw questions at 'im like boys throw rocks at a rat."

Reynolds returned Tanner's hard gaze placidly. He shifted his wad of chew again to the other side.

" 'Bout a week an' a half ago, one of Tate's riders disappeared. Young fella name of Kyle Bridges. Couple days ago, you show up with Rooster Barstow's body draped across his horse. I figure somebody tipped over a barrel of rattlesnakes, an' I'm about gatherin' 'em up."

"Sheriff, you know damn well I didn't kill the old man."

"I know that. Or at least I'm pretty sure of it. I went out an' looked at him. But there's sumpin' screwy here, and"— he lifted one meaty fist and thrust a forefinger at Tanner's chest—"you know sumpin' you ain't sayin'. I heard your story, an' I buy it, to a point. But you're holdin' back."

Tanner blinked. Of a sudden, he felt a wary respect for Reynolds. Either the man was bluffing, trying to smoke him out, or he had some kind of second sight.

He deliberated a moment longer. He shrugged. "What the hell. You're the law. I was going to tell you anyway. I just didn't want to get into a long discussion now. I'm a bit pressed for time."

"That's right," said Reynolds evenly. "I'm the law."

Tanner told him then about finding the body of the horse.

"Describe it," ordered the lawman.

"Good-looking sorrel with a blaze face. Fine animal. Damn shame."

The sheriff pondered a moment. "I ain't right sure, but I think that might've been Bridges's horse. I'll have to check on that. Bullet in the head, you say. Could it be someone put 'im down, like for a broken leg or sumpin'?"

Tanner shook his head. "I checked. He looked sound as a dollar to me. And he had all his riggin' on—saddle, scabbard. No rifle in the boot, though.

"No," continued Tanner. "He was shot deliberate. And he had been purposely hid, probably with the hope that the wolves would sniff him out and take care of the body before spring."

"Did you look around? Like for sign of the rider?"

"I did. You got to remember, the snow was deep at the time. This chinook might help clear it off a bit."

Reynolds sighed. "Well, I guess that just about puts the

dollars over Kyle Bridges's eyes. An' that ain't gonna ride well with the Tates."

"Was he a good hand?" asked Tanner.

" 'Bout like pot metal. No real iron to 'im. Thing was, it was talked about he and Miss Eleanor might be workin' toward sumpin'. An' let me tell ya, Tanner, ol' John Tate don't allow no one messin' with his daughter's happiness. Anyways, couple of weeks ago, Bridges comes up missin'. I was just kind of assumin' he had lit out on her, ya know. But you findin' his horse puts a whole different slant on things, wouldn't you say?"

With an effort, Reynolds pulled himself upright. "Well, I guess I'd better figure on ridin' up that way, anyhow. If the chinook blew up in the hills the way it did down in the valley, it may have laid sumpin' to light. That white stuff can cover a heap o' sins. But one thing about it, what's underneath always surfaces sooner or later.

"Another thing about it," he continued pointedly, "if everything bears out the way it's pointin', we got us a killer runnin' around loose."

Tanner got up off the bed. "Since I'm the outsider, I'm the most likely. Is that it?"

"No need to get worked up jus' yet," Reynolds answered nonchalantly. "Just doin' what the town pays me for. I ain't accused you of nothin' yet."

Tanner's patience was gone. He picked up his hat from the bed. "I'm late, Sheriff. If you got any more questions, I'll be back this evening." He walked to the door. As far as he was concerned, the meeting was over.

"Just one more thing, Tanner." Reynolds wheezed and lumbered with an arthritic limp after him. "I'd like to know where it is you're headed right now. Case I need to come after you."

"I'm on my way to the Tate ranch. By invitation."

Reynolds blinked. "You acquainted with the Tates, huh? Well, I guess that says sumpin' for you. Do me a favor, though, an' don't stray too far." He pivoted his bulk around to face Tanner head-on. "Above all, don't leave the valley. A move like that I'm apt to take all wrong."

"This is where I'm staying, Sheriff. And there's no one going to run me out—or lock me up."

CHAPTER 6

"YOU'RE late, Lee. I was afraid you had changed your mind about our ride."

She was looking up into his face, searching, smiling a little, bringing to life a dead winter afternoon. As far as the eye could see, the day was a sodden mass of mud and dirty snow. Tree limbs hung naked against a gray sky. The light breeze, though still warm, carried the dread of yet another storm. But to the ugliness, Lee was blind. He felt better at this moment than he had in a long, long time.

He smiled apologetically. "I was held up for a while this morning. Ran into an old friend. He took me out to look at some horses."

They walked from the Tate ranch house down a rock-strewn walkway to the stable area. When they reached the horses, he moved to help her mount. She ignored his offered hand and swung easily into the saddle. Her control over the small gray mare was firm and sure, backing the animal smoothly away from the hitching post, past Tanner's Appaloosa. She turned the mare on a short spin and then pulled up, waiting for Tanner to mount and join her.

They cut directly across country, moving at an easy lope, heading southwest, as though to the snow-covered mountains. After they had covered a mile of the sodden ground, they pulled up to a walk.

"Tell me about yourself, your family," she said. "You're from Colorado, I know."

"Oklahoma, originally. When I lost my wife and children, I loaded up my parents and we moved to Colorado. I was there for twenty years, until my folks passed away just recently."

She looked at him with curious eyes. "You never remarried, in all those years?"

He shook his head. "Thought about it once or twice, but just never got the job done."

"Losing your wife and children must have been unbearable."

"For a fact. I hurt so bad I thought I was going to die myself."

He looked up at the iron-gray sky. Slowly drifting clouds were layering themselves up for a new effort of some kind. He looked to his horse. The usually high arching neck hung low and plodding.

"If you don't mind my asking . . ." she prompted, leaving the question itself unspoken.

"It was an outbreak of cholera," he answered simply. "I was still in the army then. We hadn't quite lost it yet. I was running around the countryside trying to find horses. They were using them up as fast as I gathered them. Anyway, I got this letter from Dad. And he said don't feel bad about not being there, because there wasn't anything I could've done. That particular run of cholera took about two hundred folks from our neck of the woods."

They reached a ridge and dropped down the far side, and there the going got tougher. They hit a bog, and long tangled reeds massed like a web to snare them. When they had fought through the bog, they encountered a bed of flint, breaking here and there through the snow. Good ground, Tanner thought, for giving a horse sore feet.

When they reached solid ground again, they paused for a rest. They dismounted and let the horses pull at some scraggly clumps of yellow bunch grass poking through the snow.

"Lee, I'm sorry about your family," she said gently. "How

you must have anguished. Thank God you had your parents to help you through it."

"I probably would have gone crazy without them. But this happened almost twenty years ago, and a man goes on. I had my folks until just last year. Guess the Good Lord figured it was time for me to be on my own."

The wind, carrying a brisk chill, tugged at the fringe on her doeskin jacket and toyed with the ends of her blond hair.

She seemed more relaxed now, approachable. The icy reserve had begun to thaw, and he caught her smiling occasionally.

He asked himself again, what did he have to offer a woman of Eleanor's caliber? He was older—considerably. And considerably poorer.

On the other hand, he thought as his eyes scanned the wide expanse of terrain before them, if a man were to work a spread like this for a couple of good years, get the house fixed up nice . . .

"Lee, I need to know . . . Did Rooster suffer?"

He found her eyes filled with sadness and concern.

He meant to couch the truth, for her sake. "I reckon for the most part he was in a coma or such. When I got there he was pretty much a mess. I cleaned him up some, and he seemed to rest easy after that. When he passed away, he just went to sleep."

She nodded, and her eyes dropped, to cover the threat of tears, he thought.

"What was he doing up so high, anyway?" she asked suddenly. "He was too old to be chasing stock up that high. Why, one storm can drop five feet of snow in a night."

"It'd be my guess that's just what happened. I found his last camp. Apparently, he just made the cabin in time.

"I don't know," he continued quietly. "Maybe if I'd started across the pass a couple days earlier—if I'd found him a little earlier . . ."

"Lee," she said softly, "you did a wonderful and compassionate thing. You must never reproach yourself for something over which you had no control."

He shrugged. "Maybe you're right. He did seem like a fine old gent, though."

He gathered up the reins and stepped into the saddle. She followed suit, and they moved off at a walk.

She led the way down a long slope, through a heavily wooded area at the bottom and out onto a flat piece running a half-mile across. A wide stream at the bottom of a shallow cut wandered its way across the flat. Although the snow had not done much melting at this point, Tanner could picture the gently undulating plain covered with knee-high grass in the spring.

Resting on a slight knoll near the center of the saucer, skirted with a dozen large locust trees, stood the small, two-story ranch house.

Even from a distance, the run-down condition of the house and outbuildings was painfully apparent. As they rode near, a coyote trotted off the front porch, cast an anxious glance at the riders, and skulked off through the trees. Crumbling corrals, a low-slung, tired-looking barn, and a henhouse all showed the ravages of neglect and the elements.

"You'll have a big job just making it livable," said Eleanor.

What she had said proved to be an understatement. The interior of the house was in shambles. Bits of broken plaster clinging to the ripped wallpaper fluttered in the breeze coming from the open doors and broken-out windows. Piles of bird and animal excrement cluttered the wooden floor.

But beyond the present sad condition of the house Tanner could see a well-built and sturdy structure, built to last for many years to come.

As if reading his thoughts, Eleanor said, "I realize it doesn't look like much now, but it's got real character, don't you think? If someone were looking for a place to put down roots and raise a family, I would say this would do just fine."

She led him through the rubble into the kitchen, the main

living area of the country home. Situated as it was, on the downwind side, this room had suffered considerably less weather damage. The wooden floor had remained dry and smooth. The wallpaper, though stained, still clung to the walls intact. Except for the smell of rodent urine, the room was basically unspoiled. Tanner could see the kitchen serving as living quarters while work was being done on the rest of the house.

They finished with their inspection of the interior, tramped about outside for a time, and then returned to their horses. As they rode away, he took one last look back at the sad and lonely house.

They moved along at an easy lope, quartering their previous trail so as to give Tanner something different to look at.

At the halfway point, they pulled up to give the horses a blow, and Tanner, with a firm hand on his excitement, expressed to Eleanor his approval of the Whiteman place.

"I'm pleased, Lee. Daddy said I wasn't to talk price, but I'm sure he will work things out to your satisfaction."

The late-afternoon chill had begun to settle about them, and, looking at her, with only the light jacket for protection, Tanner wondered whether she was warm enough. He realized suddenly that she was returning his look, smiling. Had she said something he missed? he wondered.

She removed her riding glove and extended her hand. He stared at it a moment and then jerked his own glove off and seized her hand in his own big callused palm.

"Deal?" she asked, smiling.

"Deal," he answered hoarsely.

Billy Tate stood facing the whitewashed toolshed, about twenty feet away. He had used his knife to gouge the outline of a full-sized man into the shed wall. His right hand hung limp at his side, inches from his low-slung six-gun.

He rocked forward on the balls of his feet, drew his gun, and dry-fired at the figure on the wall. He paused a moment, considering, and then replaced the gun in its holster. He repeated the process several times, unhurriedly, analyzing each move. On his young face there was an expression of anger and frustration.

"Got to quit that goddamn rollin' forward each time," he growled.

With an effort he relaxed his upper body, forcing himself to breathe slowly and deeply. And then he drew the gun. He repeated this process twice more, relaxing, deep-breathing, drawing, and dry-firing.

"That's gettin' it!" A smile spread across his small, effeminate mouth. He continued the routine for several minutes, lost in concentration.

Hooves pounding the frozen crust of the scattered remains of the snow broke into his consciousness. He looked up to see his sister riding across the yard to the stable area, accompanied by that tall stranger he and Quince had brought in.

Billy watched curiously as the old wrangler emerged from the barn and took Eleanor's mare from her. The stranger tied his Appaloosa to the corral fence and, with Eleanor at his side, started toward the house. They walked close together, and they were talking in low tones. At one point, Eleanor's boot slipped on a stone. The stranger caught her before she could fall, and they laughed. Eleanor locked her arm through his as they continued up the walk. Their course would bring them within speaking distance of where Billy stood, nervously flexing the fingers of his right hand.

If Tanner was aware of the young man, he gave no indication, and this rankled Billy. A man ought to at least have respect enough to nod. As they walked past, Eleanor glanced at Billy absently, as though he might have been a bush, and continued her hushed conversation with Tanner.

Billy was already bristling over having to care for Tanner's horse the night they had brought him in. Billy wasn't no goddamn hostler. Someday at least part of this ranch would be his, and Quince and Eleanor and the rest of them had damn well better keep that fact in mind.

He watched the couple continue to the house and enter through the back door. Then he turned back to the figure of the man on the wall. *Relax. Breathe slow. Don't rock. Draw and snap.*

John Tate sat hunched behind his desk, shirt-sleeves rolled up on his forearms, black necktie loosened. He appeared tired and maybe a bit cranky. His mood brightened when the door to his study opened and Eleanor came swinging in, followed by Tanner.

Tate pushed himself from his chair and lurched around the end of the desk, hand extended.

"Lee, it's damn nice to see you again. Sit down. Sit down, my friend." He motioned Tanner to a large polished leather chair before the desk.

"Eleanor, sweetheart, will you be so kind as to fix us all some brandy? Get it from that special bottle in my bedroom. I've had a hard day, and you two are just what the doctor ordered." He called after her, "And warm the brandy, will you, dear?" He grimaced as he eased his chunky body back into his high-backed chair.

When the door closed, he said, "Well, Lee, I understand you had a visit from our sheriff earlier this afternoon."

Tanner shook his head ruefully. "I can't believe the way news gets around this valley."

Tate laughed. "Actually, Loyal Reynolds is an old friend. He happened to be out this way—"

"Did he tell you he's got his eye on me as a possible killer?"

"Oh, nonsense. All you did was find a dead horse. And you found it during the commission of a wonderful act of kindness. He can't possibly have serious suspicions regarding you—if Kyle Bridges is dead at all."

"Mr. Tate, the sheriff said Bridges and Eleanor were . . . uh . . ."

Tate looked annoyed. "Sometimes the sheriff digresses from the outlines of his job a bit too much." He pushed back in his chair. "Well, I guess it was true, after a fashion. I don't think it was nearly as serious as some would like to believe.

"Kyle Bridges was a no-good scallywag. I know. I used to have my men keep an eye on him. A few weeks ago, I found out he had a little floozy in town. He'd been keeping company with Eleanor, then riding into town and spending the night with his harlot. I told Eleanor the truth about him to discourage her from seeing him.

"And Eleanor, to her credit, said she never wanted to see him again. So really, no one was upset when he just took off. Billy—my boy Billy—he's pretty sharp. Billy figured Bridges was only after Eleanor's share of the property anyway. And I ain't so sure but what he was right."

Tate rocked forward and placed both hands on the desk top. "At any rate, you have nothing to be concerned about, Lee. Me and the sheriff, we had a talk this afternoon, and I can see his thinking, but I told him he was on the wrong track. If Bridges was killed—and we're not sure at this point that he was—what he needs to be looking for is some down-and-out saddle bum. Not a man of purpose and a man soon to be of standing in the community."

He paused and gave Tanner another smile. "Eleanor said this morning she was going to show you around the Whiteman place today. Obviously, you two have been up to something. I've not seen my daughter's cheeks this rosy in some time."

"Well," replied Tanner with a slow smile, "I wouldn't know about that, but I'm pretty excited about the Whiteman place. It has a lot of promise. It's damn near what I was looking for."

"Excellent. Well, let's not waste any time, then. I'll draw up the papers right away."

"Hold it!" Tanner laughed. "We haven't even talked price

yet. I've only got two thousand dollars in the bank, and I'm going to have to live off part of that."

Tate waved a hand as though brushing away a fly. "We'll work it out, Lee. I told you that." He opened a drawer, pulled out a single sheet of paper, and laid it on the desk. "I had some free time yesterday to do some thinking on this, and I'd like to share with you what I've come up with."

There was a soft knock. The door swung open, and Eleanor entered carrying a large silver tray laden with glasses of brandy and slices of fruitcake.

She had changed her clothes. In place of the riding togs, she now wore a pink-flowered dress with long sleeves and a lace front, buttoned up to a snug lace collar. At her throat she wore an ivory cameo. She had brushed her blond hair into a soft mass and had fastened it atop her head with carved ivory combs. Tanner gazed appreciatively, and Eleanor flashed him a tiny, rewarding smile.

Tanner noticed with a certain sadness that there were only two glasses on the tray.

As if reading his thoughts, she said, "You men are talking business. I won't intrude, but I'll see you before you leave, Lee. There is something I want to ask you." She brushed from the room, leaving her delicate scent on the air.

"Let me get into this thing, Lee," continued Tate. "I look at it this way . . . and it is only advice, mind you. If you don't like the way it lays, we'll try something else."

Tanner sipped the warm brandy and settled back comfortably. His eyes drifted lazily about the room, taking in the rich atmosphere. An intricate ship's model rode the crest of the mantel above the stone fireplace. And above that hung a large seascape depicting a sailing ship similar to the model, riding the angry tempest of a gray-green sea in the throes of a violent storm.

His gaze seemed to be led about the room, and as John Tate rummaged for a moment in a desk drawer, Tanner twisted in his chair and his eyes were drawn irresistibly to the portrait. On the wall, almost directly behind his chair, hung a painting of a beautiful woman. Recognition flashed in Tanner's eyes. It was Eleanor. But no, it was an older woman. Or was it? He squinted closely at the portrait.

"My wife," explained Tate, closing the drawer.

"I thought for a minute I was looking at Eleanor. The resemblance is uncanny."

"In the portrait she is about the age of Eleanor right now. I agree, their similarity is remarkable." Tate smoothed the forms on the desk, and Tanner, thus called back, turned to face the banker.

"We'll leave your two thousand right where it's at. That establishes your credit. The bank, on the basis of that money, can advance you operating capital and living expenses for one year. At the end of that year, you should realize some kind of profit. We can apply that profit and set up a regular payment schedule on the property and the loan for operating expenses."

Tanner shook his head incredulously. "That's a dream of a deal," he said. "A man can't lose."

Tate grinned. "That's the winner's way. The prospect of losing should not enter into it."

"There's just one thing," Tanner said. "I would like to make payments quarterly instead of yearly. With the Army as close as it is and hungry for mounts, I figure to be making money within a matter of months. It would also lessen the shock of making that one big payment each year."

"No problem," said Tate, taking up his pen. "How much do you think you could handle on a quarterly basis?"

Tanner figured in the air a moment. "How does eight hundred sound?" he asked a bit hesitantly.

"Sounds fine to me." Tate began scratching on the paper with the ink pen.

"Do you think the bank will go for it?" Tanner was still skeptical. Nothing in his life had ever come this easily.

Tate smiled indulgently. "I'll guarantee they'll go for it."

He handed the sheet of paper across the desk. "I've worked up projections on your operating costs, stocking the place, living expenses, money to fix up the house, and so on. Look it over. If you like it, come by the bank tomorrow and we'll sign the actual papers. Better yet, come out for dinner tomorrow night. Eleanor would like that."

Tanner folded the paper, thrust it into his pocket, and stood up. Tate walked him to the study door, straining to put his arm across the taller man's shoulder in a fatherly fashion.

"Whatever you do, Lee, don't take that little gal too lightly. I know I probably pamper her too much, but she's got real values and she's a strong person in her own right."

They paused in the open doorway. "Believe me, John, I do not take Eleanor lightly." Tanner hoped his voice conveyed all the sincerity he felt.

Tate smiled his pleased, elfish smile, and the two men shook hands.

Eleanor, waiting outside the door, helped Tanner into his coat. His head was swimming. The brandy, the proposed contract for his ranch in his pocket, and Eleanor Tate smiling up at him—it was overwhelming.

She stood with arms folded, a knowing and satisfied smile on her lips. "I told you Daddy would work it out."

"Yes," Tanner admitted. "You told me. I'll never doubt you or your father again."

She stood close to him, a finger tracing the decorative stitching over his coat pocket. "One week from Saturday night is the annual Tate family Christmas party. Consider this a personal invitation from the party's hostess."

"I would love to come, but . . ." Tanner stammered.

"But you think you might feel out of place?" she said gently.

He nodded. A trace of red color crept up his neck.

"You needn't be worried about that, Lee. There'll be only simple country folk, ranchers, old friends from town, people just like us. Please say you'll come." She looked up at him with pleading eyes.

Tanner admitted to himself that he was helpless to say no to her about anything, so he complied.

"Oh, good!" Like a child, she stood on her tiptoes and kissed him on the cheek. "Now, you get yourself back to town. It's not safe on the road after dark."

He smiled stupidly, turned, and stumbled for the door.

The cold air outside helped bring his mind into focus. As he moved down the pathway to the corrals, he tried to sort out the things happening to him. Normally it was his nature to question any good that came too easily.

As he rounded the toolshed, he walked into the drawn gun of Billy Tate. Instinctively, Tanner's hand dropped to the butt of his six-gun, and froze there.

Tate smiled and thumbed back the hammer. Their eyes locked, and Tanner saw the smile in the young man's eyes fade.

There was no time for thought, no time to be afraid. Tanner waited for what would probably be sudden death. There was no way he could draw before the kid pulled the trigger. And there was certainly no way Billy—or anyone— could miss at this distance.

There was a dry snap that reverberated in Tanner's ears like a cannon shot. The smile returned, the arm relaxed, and the young man lowered the gun into his holster.

Despite the cold, Tanner's face and chest were wet. He had always felt that when the time came he would face death squarely. He was not afraid to die. Yet the sudden, certain, inescapable fact, followed by the equally meaningless reprieve, had left him shaking inside.

He could think of no words to say. The kid had used him for a fool, a joke. Tanner wanted to smash that smirking face, to beat it into a pulp with the kid's own gun. Instead, he turned and walked to his horse, followed by Billy's low chuckle.

Billy watched the tall man ride away. He smiled. Now he felt good. He felt damn good. He had found a way to get respect from that man, from any man. And get it instantly. Still smiling, he started for the barn.

A white hen, seeking her roost in the growing darkness, crossed the barnyard in front of him. *Relax. Deep breath. Draw.* And snap—the hen was lifted, tossed a dozen feet against the barn wall, and came to rest in the manure, a twitching mass of white and crimson feathers.

CHAPTER 7

THE bittersweet dreams that had plagued Tanner's sleep for so many years had been swept away. In their place he rode the big proud Appaloosa across grass-covered acres, waded streams, and watched newborn foals frolic around their grazing mothers. He dreamed of a gleaming white house and the lady in the gown with the ivory cameo at her throat. And when he awoke, he wore a satisfied smile on his lips.

As befitting his mood, the sun streamed in the window of his hotel room and traced the lace patterns of the curtains on his bed covers. The room was exquisitely cold, his bed deliciously warm, and he lay there for several minutes, basking in the comfort and in his own good inner feelings. Even his brush with Billy Tate last evening lay crumpled and unimportant in a dark corner of his mind.

He threw back the covers and walked across the icy floor to the window. At this early-morning hour, the street was nearly deserted. A lone wagon rattled over the icy ruts in the street, white vapor charging from the team's nostrils. The driver huddled on the seat, bundled against the cold.

Tanner shivered and crawled into his clothes. The water in the pitcher on the washstand was crusted. He broke the ice with a knuckle and gave his face and hands a quick, perfunctory wash, vowing to treat himself to a shave at the barbershop after breakfast.

As he combed his hair in the mirror, he noticed the gash on his forehead had scabbed over nicely and most of the discoloration was gone. He grinned at his reflection. Hell, get the scars healed up, shave every now and then, start eating regular meals, and the face wouldn't be that hard to look at.

There were wrinkles, but rather than detract from the barren good looks, they seemed to lend an additional facet of character. Like the slight silvering of the dark hair at the temples.

Tanner had to turn to one side to fit the reflection of both shoulders in the mirror. The rest of the body was in equally solid condition, lean and tough. He had never pampered himself. The body he looked upon in the mirror had served him well, like a good horse, like the Appaloosa. And it had a good far piece to carry him yet.

He slipped into his fleece-lined coat and picked up his hat.

It was nearly noon when he finished his business in town. The past hour he had spent at the mill, outlining his lumber needs and making arrangements for delivery. With that out of the way, he returned to the hotel, feeling his affairs were well under way, but feeling, at the same time, a sense of pressure building. He had not forgotten that he was to have dinner at the Tates' tonight, and there was still much to be taken care of during the afternoon hours.

He had a quick lunch in the hotel's dining room, then went up to his room for his Winchester and headed for the livery stable.

Jake nickered from a stall at Tanner's approach, eager to be turned out, and stood wild-eyed while Tanner threw on the saddle.

At the edge of town, Tanner put the Appaloosa into an easy lope and pulled his collar flaps up around his ears. It was fast growing cold again. The threatened storm of last evening had passed over the valley and was at this moment depositing a fresh load of snow on the mountains and foothills. That thought brought to mind Sheriff Reynolds's comment that he might take a ride up to the pass to have a look around. Tanner shrugged. The sheriff appeared to be a wise man—wise enough not to get caught in a killing snowstorm.

By the slightly higher elevation of the Whiteman place from the other ranches in the valley, Tanner knew he could expect harsher treatment from the weather. But he didn't mind bad weather, as long as he had time to prepare.

He hoped this afternoon to be able to make a more extensive appraisal of the place, primarily the holding pens and corrals for the training stock he would soon be buying.

Tanner pulled the Appaloosa to a walk and twisted in the saddle. An animal-like warning had sent a chill up his spine. He had left the frail sunshine a ways back, and the sky was now covered over by a sheep's-wool layer of gray clouds. Ahead, a blanket of fog awaited him. He scanned his back-trail: the silent, rolling terrain, the frost-crusted tufts of buffalo grass, everything breathlessly still in the icy mist.

His gaze was pulled off to the right to a hollow filled with a stand of small locust, limbs bare and groping. In their midst, Lee thought he had detected movement, but he couldn't be sure.

He pulled the horse to a halt and stared in the direction of the trees for several long moments. He focused his eyes a little to one side, aware that a man's peripheral vision often picked up movement more readily than a head-on look. After a full minute, he concluded he had been mistaken. His horse blew, struck the frozen ground with a hoof, and then stood silent, ears up, flicking impatiently.

The fog was starting to move in. Tanner squeezed the horse's sides with his knees and moved off at a walk, still uneasy, scanning the terrain as he rode. The fog thickened, closing in and sealing off visibility until he could see only a few yards in any direction.

He arrived at the deserted ranch house a half hour later, just as the fog opened up, released him, and continued on its way down the valley. He was tying his horse at the collapsed corral when he saw the rider.

The figure must have been nearly a half-mile distant,

sitting the dark horse on a slight swell just beyond the little stream.

There were no details to be made out, only a dark figure on a dark horse. At this range, whoever it was posed no visible threat. Just the same, Tanner fought down an impulse to free his rifle from the scabbard. He watched the rider across his saddle, resting his arm on the leather and pondering the ghostlike figure.

He felt gooseflesh gripping his arms. There was something spooky in the whole situation, something sinister and menacing. Tanner recalled something from the Bible about a lone horseman as the symbol of death.

He caught himself and smiled. That's it, Tanner: play it for all it's worth. A curious cowhand had followed him, that was all.

He watched the distant figure turn about and disappear below the rise of ground. A moment later, the knoll itself was wiped away in a passing wisp of fog.

Tanner stared a moment longer, aware only of being alone, intensely alone. The icy wind soughed through the barren arms of the locusts, numbing his face and gloved fingers. A barn door moaned softly. There was a flutter of hidden wings from the loft. From somewhere within the empty ranch house a curtain or a piece of wallpaper flapped softly.

The Appaloosa bunched its shoulders and swung its head inquiringly about. Tanner slapped the big horse on the neck and collected himself.

"Little enough getting done this way, Jake, ol' boy." He had loosened the girth strap when he had stepped down, and now, on an impulse, he pulled it snug again.

It didn't take him long to size up the house with an eye to the materials he would need for fixing it up. The lumber he had ordered that morning. Window glass, plaster, and wallpaper—he would need it all. And, of course, all the usual household furnishings. In the case of the latter, he hoped to enlist the aid of Eleanor in making his selections. It might, he reasoned, save time and trouble later on.

For now, with just himself to think of, he could get by with the bare essentials. But the house must be made snug. The icy winds must be sealed out, and a good heating stove range would be needed to drive out the cold.

He took a piece of paper and the stubby pencil from his pocket and jotted down all the items and materials he would need to get started on the house. The finished list was long and would tally up to a tidy sum, but John Tate had assured him there would be money in the deal for this very thing.

The cold seemed more intense when he left the house and returned for his horse. It penetrated even his fleece-lined coat. The Appaloosa stamped, and plumes of smoke jetted from its wide nostrils.

"You and I are looking forward to the same thing, Jake," he told the horse, swinging into the saddle. "It's just too damn cold out here for gentlemen like us. Let's make us some tracks."

CHAPTER 8

TANNER arrived at the Tate ranch house just after dark and was greated warmly at the door by Eleanor herself. There was no reserve in her manner now. She took his arm boldly and drew him into the warmth of the foyer, where she divested him of coat, hat, and gloves.

"Now, listen," she whispered conspiratorily. "I want you to go directly into Daddy's study. Get all that business stuff out of the way, then we'll have the rest of the evening to enjoy."

"You make the business stuff sound like some kind of an ordeal," Tanner replied with a grin. "If the papers on the place get signed tonight, I'll become a responsible citizen and landowner again. I can't imagine the rest of the evening topping that."

"We'll see." She winked slyly. "We'll see."

His time in John Tate's study was short, almost as though it were a planned maneuver between Eleanor and her father. Over a glass of excellent whiskey, Tanner quickly reviewed the papers of the agreement. All appeared in order, and the agreement was written up exactly as Tanner had requested.

Tanner returned the documents to the desk and looked up with a broad smile.

"Suit you?" Tate asked. "It's not too late to make changes."

"It's fine as she stands," said Tanner. "Just show me where to sign."

When the paperwork was cleared away, another drink was poured. John Tate settled back in his chair, glass clutched to his barrel chest, smiling placidly.

"Does it seem things are moving pretty fast, Lee? Three,

57

four days ago you were homeless, waist-deep in a snowdrift. Now, a landowner and a businessman."

"I feel like I'm caught up in a whirlwind," Tanner answered truthfully. "The ranch, new friends, new town. It all seems to be piling up on me faster than I can soak it up."

Tate nodded. "Watching you takes me back to when I was first getting started myself. I was running full speed, never getting anything done. That's something you need to remember, Lee, a chronic complaint of a successful man—he never seems to have enough hours in the day."

He stood abruptly and walked around the desk. "Listen, I've got to run. I've a meeting in town tonight. One of those last-minute things. Remember what I said about the successful man being shorted on hours."

He extended his hand. "Remember, Lee, you get into any problems, you come and see me right away. I'll always be there to help, with advice or anything else you might need."

"I appreciate that, John," Tanner said, moved. "You've already done so much. And I'll sure try not to let you down."

Tate held Tanner's hand firmly. "I know you won't let me down, Lee." He slapped Tanner on the back and pointed him to the door. "Now, I'd better turn you loose before Eleanor has my hide." He pulled a gold watch from a vest pocket. "Oh, my God. I'm late already."

Eleanor greeted them in the large sitting room. Tate kissed his daughter on the cheek and shook Tanner's hand once more before leaving.

"I was just having some sherry," Eleanor said, closing the door behind her father. "Would you care for some?"

Tanner smiled acceptance. "Too bad your father had to leave. Doesn't he ever rest?"

"That man! Sometimes he's so infuriating. And so very obvious," she said, pouring the sherry. "This big emergency meeting was contrived, don't you know. Daddy is in the agonies of another matchmaking binge, I'm afraid." She extended to him a glass of wine. "Does that scare you, Lee?" she asked, looking him straight in the eyes.

"Scare me? Hell, it tickles me to death," Lee answered with a short laugh. "He's been pretty successful with most of his schemes, I gather. Here's hoping his luck holds out."

She touched his glass with her own and smiled.

After a sumptuous dinner served by Charlotte, they had coffee in the parlor before a softly burning fireplace. Tanner and Eleanor talked in relaxed, easy tones about nothing. About spring and Eleanor's favorite flower bulbs. About the town of Sweetwater and all the committees and organizations Eleanor had a hand in.

"When your father leads in the community," she told Tanner, "you have no choice but to be involved—to a degree, at least. I don't mind really, but I don't crave it, either."

"The burden of the rich," Tanner intoned indulgently.

"Don't scoff. You might find yourself facing these same burdens one day."

He smiled and shook his head. "I'm not much of a social animal. Too many rough corners."

She looked at him thoughtfully. "We can smooth those out, I'm sure." She smiled at that and hurried on. "Certain things are expected of the wealthy. People look up to you. And," she canted her head to one side, "you'll find out people make certain concessions to you."

"So I've noticed. Your father had no trouble finding me a ranch. Or getting the bank to approve my loan. I'd say I'm adequately impressed."

Eleanor looked at him, he felt, as if he'd missed her point.

They were silent a moment, and when she spoke next her words were couched in an indifference that only later struck him as odd.

"Incidentally," she said slowly, "we've had some news. This afternoon, Loyal Reynolds rode in. He and Davis stopped by on their way back to town. They had ridden up to the pass."

"I figured Reynolds would be headed up that way," said Tanner, curious.

"They found him," she said, matter-of-factly. "They found Kyle, you know."

"They found him?" Tanner repeated senselessly. Something akin to fear tugged at his stomach. Was Bridges alive, then? He had not forgotten the sheriff's words—that this was the man, this Kyle Bridges, whom Eleanor had at least considered for marriage. Was he coming back, to pick it all up again?

"Yes," she said. "He was quite dead. They found him close to where you found the dead horse. He had been shot—like the horse."

Relief and shame swept over him together. At least he wouldn't have to worry about Kyle Bridges and Eleanor.

"Your father told you about the horse?" Tanner asked.

"Oh, yes. And he mentioned at the same time the strong possibility that Kyle might be dead."

"Did he tell you the sheriff had his rope set for me?"

She laughed lightly. "Yes, he told me that too. But, as Daddy told you, you needn't worry about that. Daddy talked to Loyal. It's all taken care of."

A shadow passed over her face, soft and lovely in the candlelight.

"Lee, perhaps this would be a good time for us to talk about Kyle. He courted me for a time, you know."

"You must be feeling pretty bad about now. Maybe we should cut the evening short." But the last thing he wanted to do was leave her to the memories of another love.

She looked quickly at him. "Oh, no. Really, I'm fine. I don't know what you heard about Kyle and me, but it was over long before he left the ranch. Really it was." She laughed. "I suppose Loyal told you that Kyle and I were deeply involved. Loyal's an impossible gossip."

Tanner grinned, unable to mask his relief. "He did happen to mention something to that effect, yes."

"Well," she said, and she turned on one of her loveliest smiles. "All of that was long over before tonight. Right now I'm as free as a tumbleweed."

"Eleanor, you may just regret saying that."

Her smile faded. "No. I really don't think I will."

She stood up suddenly and reached for his hand.

"Come with me," she said softly. "I want to show you something. One more way the rich spoil themselves."

She led him from the parlor, across the hall and into her father's study. Beneath the portrait of her mother, she pushed gently on a seam in the paneling. The oak panels accordioned from the middle to each side, exposing an alcove ten feet deep and maybe fifteen feet in length.

The walls of the little room were a showcase of firearm relics garnered from the Civil War and before.

On the two end walls hung grimed and tattered flags of either faction in the war, authentic battlefield standards, to be sure. Arranged in rows beneath the flags, and filling the back wall in its entirety, was the most impressive array of war weapons Tanner had ever seen. Resting on burnished brass hooks were the scarred, oiled rifles used by either side. There were American-made muskets and a British Enfield, adaptable to the American .58-caliber bullet. A Sharps .54, in near mint condition, caught Tanner's eye.

Swords, sabers, bayonets, and daggers of every size and weight gleamed wickedly in the lamplight.

Inserted in spaces too small for either sword or rifle was John Tate's arsenal of handguns: smooth-bore "horse pistols," dragoons, and five- and six-shot revolvers of the type used prior to the self-contained metal cartridge. Tanner took one from its hooks and examined it closely. The revolvers from this era required each chamber in the cylinder to be loaded with powder and bullet and then tamped down with a small ramrod built into the weapon.

"I'm amazed," he said at last. "I've been in your father's study at least twice, and I had no idea any of this was here."

He looked down at Eleanor with quick alarm. "Maybe he didn't mean for me to see this."

"Of course he did," she answered, slipping an arm beneath his. "It was Daddy's idea to have me show it to you. As to why he didn't show it before, he probably felt the time was too short. One needs time to soak it up."

He replaced the pistol on the wall and took down several other pieces, hefting them, working their action, sighting down the barrels.

He squinted through the sights of the comparatively shorter-barreled Sharps.

"Wonder how many Johnny Rebs have been admired over the top of this thing," he mused sadly.

She took the heavy rifle from him, handling it with ease, placed it to her shoulder, and pointed the muzzle at him.

"Does it look familiar?" she asked with a mischievous smile.

Tanner blinked and took a step backward. "Didn't your father teach you about pointing guns at folks?" He said it as lightly as possible. "Unless, of course, you intend to shoot them."

She replaced the rifle on the wall and smiled. "I'm sorry. It was a bad joke. And I've certainly been taught better than that. Old Rooster saw to that."

She stepped up to him. "Seen enough?"

Tanner nodded. "I guess for now. And thank you. I would like to see it again when your father's here. There's got to be some interesting stories behind some of those pieces."

"That would be an excellent way for the two of you to get better acquainted."

She returned the panels to their closed position and led the way from the study. As Tanner followed her from the room, he paused, hand on the door, and glanced back. Something in the portrait of Eleanor's mother had caught his eye.

The woman in the portrait was a bit older than Eleanor was now, and the nose a bit sharper. The eyes were captivating. Not pretty. Not really attractive at all. An unusual thing for the eyes of a beautiful woman. Hypnotizing; bewitching would be more accurate. But they were something else also . . . critical. Sharply and unforgivingly critical. They were . . .

"Come on, poke-along," Eleanor called to him, a quizzical expression on her face. "Was there something else, Lee?"

"No. Just gathering wool, I guess." He followed her to the parlor for more coffee.

Glancing at the mantel clock, Tanner was alarmed at the hour.

"I've got a big day tomorrow," he said, rising.

She looked genuinely saddened. "Oh, must you leave? It's been the most relaxing and wonderful evening."

"I'll agree to that," he replied sincerely. "I can't remember when I've had a finer evening."

At the door, she helped him into his coat. "You won't forget? One week from Saturday night?"

Tanner accepted his hat from her. He grinned. "I might be able to stay away that long. But I wouldn't push it much past that."

CHAPTER 9

SHE grabbed his arm and pulled him out of the swirling snow into the warm foyer, where she helped him out of his coat.

"How nice you look. And so—so dashing!"

Tanner smiled proudly. He knew how he looked. Hadn't he checked himself in the mirror a dozen times before leaving the hotel? In all modesty, he had to agree with her. He had spent way too much money just the day before on a new black suit. He damn well better look nice.

"You're not exactly an eyesore yourself," he said with lame gallantry. Every compliment he could think of had the dismal ring of comparing her to fine horseflesh. So he settled finally for saying simply, "You look mighty fine."

She smiled and did a quick twirl to show off her gown. It was low-cut and made of material so white it hurt the eyes, accented around the top and bottom of the skirt with tiny red ribbons tied in the shape of dainty rosebuds.

If Tanner had run across a woman in a saloon wearing a dress this revealing, he would immediately have taken her for a professional. In the lavish home of John Tate and on the body of Eleanor Tate, the gown was tasteful and elegant.

She slipped an arm possessively through his. "Come along," she urged. "I want to show you off. There are people here that you must meet."

As she led him into a sea of brightly colored gowns, somber black suits, and tinkling laughter, a choking sensation rose up from Tanner's stomach, squeezing off his wind, numbing his vocal cords.

The room was draped with green pine boughs and silver

tinsel, and in a corner by a large window, complete with brightly colored ornaments and a hundred small unlit candles, stood a very large Christmas tree.

Eleanor led him first to the punch bowl, a large crystal affair with a pinkish concoction. "You'll love this," she intimated, filling a dainty crystal cup and passing it to him. "It's an old family recipe. I'll admit I've taken a few liberties with it—added a few twists of my own, you might say."

Tanner looked warily at the cup in his hand. "Will I be able to find my way home after this?"

She laughed, and the sparkle in her voice turned the heads of those nearby. Tanner noticed several adoring smiles.

She took his arm and led him among the guests, introducing each in intimate tones as though they were all relatives of some distinction or another.

Most, Tanner gathered, were business or community leaders from Sweetwater, John Tate's banking partners and colleagues, and shop owners.

Although there were two or three ranchers present, conspicuously absent—at least to Tanner—were Andy Farley and his daughter.

Tanner was surprised that Sheriff Reynolds was present. He caught a glimpse of the large man, elbowing his way through the crowd, maneuvering for the punch bowl.

Reynolds looked somehow out of place in his ill-fitting suit, but his red cheeks and the twinkle in his eyes indicated he felt at home and was quite obviously having a good time. Tanner caught the sheriff's eye and nodded pleasantly.

As Eleanor led him about, Tanner shook hands, exchanged pleasantries, and tried to devise some quick method whereby he might remember at least some of the avalanche of names. The faces were coming at him so rapidly that they were beginning to blur. Tanner looked suspiciously at the empty cup in his hand.

"Well, I think that's about it," Eleanor said at last. "Let's find us a nice safe nook or cranny and enjoy our punch."

She looked at his glass and then up into his flushed face with motherly reproval. "I say, it looks as though you've already started enjoying your punch."

Tanner shrugged. "I get nervous when I meet people."

At the punch bowl, they talked a few minutes with Loyal Reynolds. Eleanor excused herself and hurried off to greet some late arrivals, leaving Tanner and the sheriff to guard the punch bowl.

"Pretty little thing, ain't she?" Reynolds commented, and Tanner noticed, to his revulsion, the man was speaking around a quid of tobacco. Although he rolled an occasional cigarette for himself, chewing was a form of tobacco use Tanner found unappealing and downright nasty.

"They don't come any prettier," he agreed, wondering if the sheriff had devised some secret method for spitting. In their elegant surroundings, he found the alternative too disgusting to consider.

"You two becoming a real item, I hear."

"I don't know about that. But things seem to be pretty comfortable between us." He was eyeing the sheriff speculatively.

"Sumpin' wrong?" Reynolds asked casually.

"Yeah. Where the hell you spittin'?"

Reynolds grinned and looked around mysteriously. "Promise you won't tell on me? They might just bounce my butt out of here." He pulled something from a side pocket. It was a small tin can, smashed nearly flat to ride unobtrusively in the coat pocket.

"Like this," he said. He turned his back quickly to the room. Tanner heard a quick, sluicing sound. The sheriff turned around, grinning.

"Pretty smart," Tanner said blandly. "I'd be careful who I bump into, though."

"Yeah. And a body never wants to run carryin' one of these things, either."

They grinned at each other and turned back to watch the

goings-on. Tanner was taking another sip of punch when he caught, across the rim of his glass, a pair of eyes boring into his own. Billy Tate lounged in an open doorway, glass in hand. On his arm was a lovely young girl; on his lips was the same insolent smile he had worn when Tanner last saw him.

Tanner lowered his own glass and glared at the young man.

Tate, still smiling, raised his free right hand and pointed his index finger, like the barrel of a pistol, taking aim at Tanner's head. He let his thumb snap forward like the falling hammer of a six-gun.

Grinning, Billy Tate mouthed the silent word, "Bang," and he and the girl laughed together. They each raised their glasses in a silent toast to Tanner, and then turned and disappeared through the doorway, leaving Tanner with jaws clinched, insides churning.

Tanner choked down his anger with a sip of punch and turned back to the proceedings.

Eleanor had been drafted by loud acclaim to play the piano, and she had just seated herself prettily on the bench, sweeping her gown around her like a nest. In agreeing to perform, she had displayed no false reluctance or shyness. Tanner marveled at her splendid grace with people as they crowded around the piano.

Someone made a request for a song, and she launched immediately into a stylish and flowery rendition of an old Christmas carol.

Everyone joined in but Tanner and Reynolds. They continued their visit, leaning close to be heard above the singing.

On Tanner's mind was Kyle Bridges. "Hear you made it up to the pass," he said.

"That's right," answered the sheriff. "Chinook done us some real good. Snow level was down to about two feet. Real easy going."

"Eleanor told me you found Bridges."

The sheriff looked at him for a long moment. "I don't

ordinarily discuss a case in idle conversation, but I dropped by and shared the news with the Tates for obvious reasons. I'll talk to you just 'cause you're kind of involved."

"You still think I had something to do with it?" Tanner asked.

Reynolds was thoughtful for a moment. "I truly don't know. John Tate vouches for you. But then again, how long has he known you, and how much does he know about you? You see what I'm sayin'?"

Tanner nodded. "Bridges was murdered, and someone's guilty. As far as you know, besides Bridges, only me and the old man was up there?"

"That's right. You got the picture. Just you an' Rooster. An' it's hard for me to picture that old fart gunnin' anyone. He was harmless as a fly. As it stands, I don't have proof enough to point a finger at anyone." He regarded Tanner's sober face. "If it means anything, Tanner—an' officially it don't mean a damn thing—I'm kind of inclined to believe you're in the clear. Call it gut feeling."

For a time they listened to the music, Tanner lost in thought, the sheriff nodding his head and tapping his feet and partaking liberally of the punch bowl.

"For argument's sake," said Tanner, "let's just leave me out of the picture totally, okay? Do you think the old man was aware of Bridges's being up on the pass?"

Reynolds shrugged. "Like you said, tracks around where you found the horse seemed to belong to the old man's mare. We found Bridges's body stuffed up under a cut bank with some dirt pulled down on top of him. Bullet between the eyes, just like the horse."

"You said you don't think the old man had it in him to gun anyone. Consider this—do you think maybe somebody else could've killed Bridges and the old man just hauled him and his horse up there, like maybe to get rid of the evidence?"

Reynolds appeared agitated. "I said I figured you had a

right to know about finding the body," he said. "I don't recall takin' you on as a deputy."

Tanner lapsed into silence, but not before he noticed the thoughtful gleam in the sheriff's eyes.

Someone requested that Eleanor sing alone. She began a slow-moving, touching song, a lover's lament.

Tanner listened with the others, and he reflected upon what seemed to be taking place. How could he dare to believe all this? How dare he stand here, hopeful that Eleanor might want to share her life with him? He looked at the crowd, gathered about her like a queen. He didn't fit in with them. They were a part of her world. This world. Here and now. He had had it in mind to propose marriage to her, but how could he hold out hope that she would accept the likes of him?

Oh, she had encouraged him. From a cold beginning, she had turned friendly, warm even. But women like Eleanor needed diversion. Maybe that is what he was to her—a male interest to attend to her for a while. There had been others— Bridges, for one. Maybe others among the men right in this room.

When the song ended, he joined sadly in the applause. He felt Reynolds's elbow jab sharply into his ribs.

"If that's what you call comfortable with each other," the sheriff muttered in Tanner's ear, "I'd say you'd better make plans on stayin' comfortable for a good long spell."

"What the hell's that supposed to mean?" Tanner asked against the noice of the applause.

"I s'pose you didn't notice she sang that song right at you?"

Tanner looked about, perplexed. She had asked him to wait in the study, and here he stood, alone, listening to the muted sounds of the party. He felt strange, but good, if a bit unsettled.

He looked down at his empty punch glass. Empty again. "You sneaky little bastard," he muttered.

Several bottles of assorted spirits stood along a side bar. He considered a moment and was helping himself to some brandy when the door to the study opened and Eleanor stepped in.

She closed the door quickly behind her and then leaned back against it. A few gleaming yellow strands drifted across her flushed, damp cheeks. Her eyes sparkled with vitality. She placed a hand on her bosom and laughed breathlessly.

"I was lucky to get out of there alive," she said, panting. "I think I danced with every man in there, all in the last five minutes."

"I can't blame them for wearing you out," he said from across the room. "You look wonderful out there."

She smiled, left the door, and crossed to him. "Not quite everyone. I didn't dance with everyone. You never asked me."

Tanner looked down into his glass. "Good enough reason for that, I guess. I don't know how." He felt his face turn hot. "Just never got around to learning."

"Don't be embarrassed," she said gently. "Dancing's not so much. Some men don't have the time or the chance to learn. Anyway, I have just the solution." She stepped up to him, took his glass from him, and set it on the bar. "I can teach you in no time."

"Now, hold on . . . ," he stammered.

"Listen to the music." She tilted her head prettily to one side. Sounding far away but reasonably clear was the tinkle of the piano. They had drafted a new pianist, and whoever it was labored out a gentle, if at times discordant, waltz.

"That will be just perfect," she said. She took his hand and led him to the center of the room. She posed him into the dance position. His right hand rested clumsily on her waist, his eyes on his feet. They started off.

Three or four awkward turns and then a surprised grin spread across his face. "Hey, I'm dancin'!"

Soon he was stepping out a little more boldly, gradually

taking the lead away from her and noticing her prideful smile when he finally took his eyes off his feet.

"You're sensational!" she exclaimed. "See, I told you. You have perfect, natural grace."

He was genuinely sorry when the waltz ended. When the piano started up again, the tune this time was a schottische, and though Eleanor coaxed him to try a few of the more intricate steps, he was soon scraping and stumbling and again feeling very foolish.

"Do you mind?" he finally asked piteously, his arms still about her.

"You've done very well. You don't have to learn it all in one night." She didn't try to release herself from his grasp, but looked steadily up into his eyes, a strange smile on her lips.

It seemed the most natural thing in the world to do. He kissed her.

She responded by pressing her firm body close to his. And when he finally released her, she pulled his face down once more and kissed him insistently and with a passion that made him dizzy.

"We need to talk," she breathed. She clasped his hand and led him to a leather settee. When they were seated facing each other, she held his big hands in her own soft small ones and looked intently into his eyes.

"Do you love me, Lee?"

"More than anything," he answered huskily. "It's been such a short time," he managed, "but you're the best thing that's ever come into my life."

She smiled, and her eyes glistened. "I feel the same way about you, darling. Now, the question is, what are we going to do about it?"

He paused. "Well, I guess . . ." he said slowly. "I guess we ought to do what most folks do about it. I mean . . ."

She was suddenly smiling at him, blue eyes sparkling.

"Eleanor, I . . . I'd like you to marry me," he blurted.

It seemed an eternity before those perfect lips parted and

the words floated forth. "There," she murmured. "Was that so hard?"

He grinned. "A lot easier than learning to dance."

She laughed and kissed him on each cheek.

"Well?" he demanded, suddenly brave, holding her by the shoulders. "It's customary to give an answer, either yes or no."

"Oh, yes!" she cried happily, hugging him. "Yes, yes, yes. Oh, Lee, we'll be so happy!"

She released him suddenly, looking startled. "Wait here, darling. I'll be right back." She leaped to her feet and fled from the room.

Tanner, his mind ablaze and his knees suddenly feeling like water, lurched to his feet and made his way to the bar. If ever he needed a drink, it was now.

He had just poured a generous dollop into his glass when the door burst open and Eleanor entered, followed by John Tate.

Tate brushed past his daughter and crossed the room, his hand extended. "By God, Lee! Eleanor has just told me the news. I can't say when I've been more pleased." He wrung Tanner's hand with surprising strength. Tanner noticed with some surprise there were actual tears in the little man's eyes. "Yes, sir, this is just wonderful. Calls for a drink, I would say." He swiped at his eyes quickly, embarrassedly with the back of his hand.

"You're about a half-minute late with that idea, John," said Tanner, tipping his glass.

"No no," said Tate, sounding near frantic. "This calls for something special. Eleanor, you run out and tell Roscoe to get a case of champagne from the cellar. I'm going to have a quick chat with Lee. Oh God, this is wonderful!"

When the door closed, Tate turned to Tanner. "There's something I want to give to you, Lee," he said solemnly. He walked to the large steel safe in the corner behind his desk and maneuvered himself painfully down to his knees before the safe's dial.

"You're the first of Eleanor's men friends that I feel is worthy of this," he explained as he worked the combination.

He swung open the heavy steel door and rummaged about in a tin box within. He apparently found what he wanted immediately, for he closed the tin box, secured the safe door, and straightened up.

Red-faced and breathless, he said, "This belonged to Eleanor's mother." He held a silver ring with a massive diamond. "Everything I bought for that woman was the best I could afford. No junk."

He placed the ring in Tanner's hand. "Now, I want you to give this to Eleanor for her engagement ring." He grinned and poked Tanner in the ribs. "What you do about the wedding ring is your own business. Personally, I favor a simple gold band, and I think Eleanor would like that too. But that's up to you and Eleanor." He paused a moment. "Well, Lee, I'd just like to say again how pleased I am. Welcome to the Tate family."

They stood alone in the foyer. Eleanor nestled against Tanner's chest, the engagement ring on her finger. Inside, the party continued its celebration, made the merrier for the announcement by her father of Eleanor's engagement, and further embellished, doubtless, by the arrival of a case of champagne.

Tanner was not drunk. At least, he didn't think so. But he was not himself right now, either. This night was made of dream stuff, and he would need days, maybe weeks for his head to clear.

"I think June would be nice, don't you?" Eleanor asked, raising her face and looking up questioningly. "June is a beautiful time to be married."

"I don't know," Tanner said doubtfully. "That's a long time

to have to wait. How about Easter? That'll give you three months to get ready."

"I don't think so, darling. I'm going to have the gown made in San Francisco. Relatives will need time to make their own arrangements. Many will have a long way to come." She hugged him for the hundredth time. "Lee, it's going to be so perfect, so grand. The whole county will be talking about our wedding. Daddy said no expense will be spared."

Tanner gave her a mock frown. "I wish to hell we didn't have to go through so much hoopla. But," he added quickly, "you're worth it, I guess. Maybe a bit more. Listen, honey, I'm just a country boy, and I get a little nervous about these social affairs."

"After it's over, you'll change your mind about that. You'll see. This will be one of our dearest memories when we're old."

She took his hand, kissed the big knuckles, and looked up with pleading eyes. "Please, Lee, indulge me on this one thing. And then I'll promise to be the best, most obedient wife ever.

"By the way, darling," she said brightly. "It's not too soon for you to be thinking about who you would like as your best man. Is there anyone in the valley you know well enough for that?"

"I got just the pigeon in mind," said Tanner, smiling at the thought. "As a matter of fact, I might just be able to return him the favor one day soon when he and Carrie step into the same harness."

She looked up suddenly. "You're not speaking of Troy Sams?"

"Why, yes," he said, surprised. "He and I knew one another in Colorado."

"You don't say so," she murmured, nestling her face against his chest.

"You know the gent, I take it. What do you think, honey? Is he deservin' of the high privilege of standin' up with me?"

"Oh, yes. He will do just fine."

Because her head rested upon his chest, he could not see the hard glint enter her blue eyes.

CHAPTER 10

TROY Sams whooped and slapped his coiled lariat at the hammerheaded gelding and turned the big horse down off the bank. Ahead of him, and off to the west, Tanner was coaxing with wild yells another fierce-eyed gelding up through the draw.

Tanner had lost sight for a moment of the rest of the bunch, but he wasn't worried. The horses up ahead were older and more settled, and his last glimpse caught them trotting calmly around and over the snow-crusted rocks and limbs lining the bottom of the draw.

He looked up at the sky. More snow coming. But it wouldn't matter now. A half hour more would bring them in, and then it could snow till it covered the peaks of hell.

Tanner was pleased with every one in the bunch. He couldn't help but make money off the deal. Angus McIntosh, because he did not have the hay to spare to feed them through the winter, had accepted an offer from Tanner for just a little better than half their actual worth.

They were rough-string material, the old man had warned him, horses the average cowhand couldn't ride or wouldn't take the time to break thoroughly.

"I got no one to do my breakin'," McIntosh had lamented. "I'm going to keep my workin' stuff and some yearlings, and you can have the rest. And God help ye! 'Cause they're a rank lot, every goddamn one of them."

Tanner had ended up with fifteen geldings, all under six years, and three fine-lined brood mares. He had felt almost guilty as he counted out the cash money into the old man's palm.

"Ye be a horse breaker, huh?" said McIntosh. "Well, tell me, if ye ever have time on the billet, I got me one of them fancy carriages ordered for me missus. Would ye be interested in breakin' out for me a pair to pull the rig?"

McIntosh was seventy-eight years old, a gnarled stick of a man, barely reaching Tanner's shoulder. Once-red hair was now a roan mane, sweeping nearly to the shoulders, framing a face as weathered and browned as the leather tobacco pouch he carried. He was rumored to be, next to John Tate, the wealthiest rancher in the valley.

A look into those steel-blue eyes made Tanner hesitate a moment, wondering if the deal for the horses he had struck with this old man would taste as sweet in the morning.

Tanner shook the old man's hand. "I'll be busy for a while with these. When I get them squared away, you can bring the pair around and I'll see what I can do with them."

Sams had given up his day off to help Tanner move the horses. It was a four-hour drive from the McIntosh ranch to Tanner's place, and the day was nearly spent when they topped out of the arroyo and moved out onto open ground within sight of the ranch buildings.

The horses settled into a resigned walk, calm and purposeful, sensing maybe that the end of the journey lay just ahead. Tanner settled back into the saddle, enjoying feelings of peace and satisfaction, a man well on his way to fulfilling a dream.

John Tate, God bless him, had seen to it that everything was going off without a hitch. He'd sent Tanner two carpenters, who had nearly completed their task. In the six weeks since the papers were signed, the desolate house and outbuildings had undergone a transformation that had amazed even Tanner. There were new pole corrals, which Tanner himself had installed, and a reroofing and general snugging up of the barn. The house, while still littered with scrap building material, was now a tight, warm fortress against the snow and wind.

Tanner had at first felt some reluctance at the lengths to which Tate had gone to get things moving. But Tate's assurance that all was being worked out in accordance with the terms of the contract settled his mind. Any further misgivings had been swept away by the embraces of Eleanor.

He savored again the way she had looked the night of the Christmas party, when they had stood alone in the foyer. At that moment, Lee Tanner's life had finally come together.

It was there, in one still instant, that he had expressed to Eleanor his surprise that she had actually agreed to marry him.

"It's meant to be, that's all." She'd raised one eyebrow and fiddled with the collar of his crisp, white shirt. "I think I knew it would turn out this way right after you bumped into me in the hallway upstairs. Maybe not in a way which I could put into words, but I'm sure I knew it in my heart."

Now Tanner charged the Appaloosa at a mare lagging behind the rest of the bunch.

But there had been that strange, almost nightmarish afternoon on Sunday, the day after the party. A ragged afternoon, when it looked for a moment as if the whole thing might unravel.

They had just finished dinner, and John Tate had excused himself to take a nap. Tanner and Eleanor were left alone in the parlor. They embraced.

After a time, he released her and they sat close together, her fingers laced into his.

"Things will be better now," she said. She had voiced the words with almost a sigh of relief. "I get lonely at times, Lee. I really need you."

"Somehow I can't imagine you ever being lonely." He kissed her on the brow, and she nestled her blond head into the hollow between his neck and shoulder.

Suddenly there was a scuffing noise behind them, and they lifted their heads in unison.

In the doorway stood Billy Tate, a wolfish grin on his

handsome face. In one hand he held a chicken leg. His mouth was smeared with grease. He lounged against the doorjamb and surveyed the couple on the sofa, chewing thoughtfully.

"Sorry I didn't get home in time for dinner, little sister," he said after a moment, "but I see you and Dad had plenty of company." He pushed away from the doorway and walked slowly over to the fireplace, threw the chicken leg into the ashes, and turned to face Tanner.

"Sure as hell didn't take you long to establish yourself," he said to Tanner, the grin turning into a broad, unfriendly smile. "Seems like just yesterday we rode you in with a rifle up your backside. Look at you now—all snuggled up with my sweet sister here as your bride-to-be. An' with a ranch of your own. Never mind that it was furnished by my old man. A cowhand could do a lot of snugglin' for a setup like that."

Tanner pulled free from Eleanor's grasp and rose quickly to his feet. Eleanor looked first up at Tanner, eyes wide, and then at her brother.

"Billy, stop it!" she ordered. "Leave this room at once!"

Billy sneered. "Why? If we're going to be family, me an' Tanner better have all our cards on the table. He's lookin' for a meal ticket, an' you're the first course."

"Shut up!" Eleanor shrieked. She left Tanner's side and confronted her brother. "It's not like that! Don't you dare interfere in my life!"

Billy blinked in the face of her quick fury and leaned back too quickly against the mantel, striking his elbow and wincing.

With an effort he steeled himself and forced the self-assured smile back onto his taut lips.

"My dear sister," he intoned sweetly, "you know Kyle didn't run off on my account. And even Troy found Miss Carrie a bit more of a woman than you." As Billy spoke he eased himself to one side where an overstuffed armchair would separate him from Eleanor's mounting fury.

Eleanor's mouth opened, a flush crimsoned her fair cheeks, and she stood helpless, clinching her small fists.

Tanner rushed to her and put a protective arm about her waist.

"If you want to insult someone, Billy, I'm your man. I don't know why you dislike me, but whatever it is, we can settle it between us. But from now on you're to leave Eleanor alone. You got that?"

"How I talk to my sister is none of your goddamn business, Tanner. And as far as settling matters with you, I'll take care of that in my own good time." He faced Tanner, eyes level, unafraid. "You're not the first to be taken in, Tanner. Her idea is to get a good strong man in here, get him into the old man's good graces, and then squeeze me out of my share of the place when the old man dies. She knows it would take a strong man to do it, because I'm a strong man. Bridges was weak, Tanner. He thought he'd found easy pickin's with my sister, but all it got him was a bullet between the eyes. You're weak too. I can tell."

"There's a big difference between weakness and restraint, Billy. You'd do well to learn to tell them apart. Could save your life someday."

Billy's eyes flashed angrily. This saddle bum was talking to him like he was a kid. He started to reply, when he noticed a strange light in Tanner's eyes that had not been there before.

"You say I'm weak, kid. I'll make you a deal." Tanner moved closer, and his tall frame loomed over Billy, forcing him to look up to meet Tanner's eyes. "You take that gun off, or leave it on, either way. It's up to you. We'll go outside right now. Like you said, we'll put our cards on the table. Hell, we'll drag out the whole goddamn deck."

Billy eased sideways away from Tanner. Billy was not much taller than Eleanor, and he preferred facing men from a distance because he detested looking up to any man.

"When we meet, Tanner—" Billy's threat was cut short by the soft voice of John Tate.

Tate stood in the doorway. "Go on to bed, Billy," he ordered softly.

Billy stared a moment and swallowed, a young colt ready to break free.

"I said go to bed, Billy. You've carried this far enough."

Billy gave Tanner a last evil glance and then turned and rushed past his father.

John Tate lumbered over to the fireplace and put his arm around Eleanor's waist.

He turned to Tanner. "What can I say, Lee? Billy's grown up a spoiled brat. I happened to be walking down the hall and heard some of the things he said to you and to Eleanor. I can only say I'm sorry. His perspective is very distorted."

"No need to apologize," Tanner answered through clinched jaws. "Didn't hurt my feelings." He looked at Eleanor. "I'm worried about her, though."

Eleanor forced a smile, but both men could see that she was drained white and that her hands, toying with the front of her dress, were trembling.

Tate said, "Billy makes Eleanor sound like a scheming spinster. I assure you that is not the case. In the past few years, she's kept company with several men. All open and aboveboard. None of them have measured up. At least not until you came along."

Tanner said sincerely, "I consider myself the luckiest man in the world. I put no stock in anything Billy said. He's a young pup who's been doing a lot of stewing in his own juices. It happens that way sometimes. I'm sure we'll work it out, John."

He chose this time to take his leave. Despite the cold, he declined Tate's offer to put him up for the night. Eleanor, he felt, needed time to regain her composure.

As he made his way through the icy wind, returning to town that night, his thoughts returned to the rider who had dogged his trail two weeks earlier. Could it have been Billy? And more devastating still, could gun-happy Billy have eliminated Bridges, who he thought was too close to becoming an heir to the Tate inheritance?

The thought had remained with Tanner ever since, sticking in the back of his head like a burr under a saddle blanket. And now, six weeks later, as he and Sams hazed the horses into the main holding pen, Tanner felt his eyes drawn to the distant knoll where the rider had stood.

When the horses were secure and the gate fastened, Sams moved his ungainly bay alongside Tanner's horse.

"You're well started now, Lee," Sams remarked, placing a wad of chew in his cheek. "I can't believe the work that's been done around the place in so short a time." He eyed admiringly the new corrals, the holding and training pens—all made with new poles and white, clean lumber.

Tanner noted with a warm, satisfied glow Eleanor's small gray mare tied to the hitch rack in front, cinch hanging slack. "We might've just blundered into a home-cooked meal, my friend," he said with a smile.

Sams, too, had noticed the mare.

"I guess I'd better be movin' along, Lee," he said, suddenly sober.

"No such thing. Not after the day you've put in. You gotta try Eleanor's cooking. You and Carrie will be joining us a lot, if I know women."

Sams appeared uneasy. "Really, Lee . . ."

It came back to Tanner then, the remark Billy had made that night about Eleanor and Troy. In the heat of the moment, Tanner had skipped over the comment because he was caught up in his concern for Eleanor and his anger at Billy. Now the full impact hit him.

"Aw, yeah," he said in an anguished tone. For a moment he and Sams looked at each other in silence. "Well, I guess you'd better tell me about it," he said dismally. "I gotta know."

"I guess so," agreed Sams, equally miserable. "Really, Lee,

I should've said something before but . . . I guess I was afraid, or embarrassed."

They had dismounted and leaned now with backs against the new pole corrals. Lee pulled at a sliver of one of the poles, digging with a restless thumbnail into the soft wood.

Sams looked away. "I don't want to get you mad. I seen you mad."

"Troy, we're both grown men—getting older by the minute. We ain't got time to mince words. Let's have it."

Sams shrugged. "Lee, it's not so simple. Not just what you think." His fingers shook as he rolled a cigarette. "There's something you need to know. An' me, bein' your friend—an' things being as they are—well, I guess it's my job to tell you."

"Goddamn it, Troy. Either speak up or crawl back up on your horse. I don't have time for this."

"I guess you figured out by now that I courted Eleanor for a time."

"I gathered that much," Tanner replied impatiently.

"It wasn't exactly a great courtship." Sams hesitated again, as though a mighty struggle was taking place within.

At last he said quietly, "I'm the one what broke it off, Lee."

Tanner looked at his friend closely. "Now, that strikes me as pretty strange, Troy. Saying nothing against Carrie, you telling me you dumped the richest and the most beautiful girl in the valley? Goddamn, Troy. I got to ask why."

"She tried to kill me."

"Now, just a goddamn minute . . ."

"It's true. She tried to blow my head off."

CHAPTER 11

THE next morning, Tanner was up well before daybreak. He rolled from the lonely cot in his icy room off the kitchen and dragged himself and his clothes into the kitchen where he dressed by the feeble warmth of the stove.

Throughout the long day, his conversation with Troy Sams returned to haunt him. Of the things Sams had said concerning Eleanor, Tanner totally disregarded the talk of insane rages, murderous jealousy, possessiveness—traits that simply did not go with the Eleanor he knew and loved.

Tanner had managed to hang on to his temper—he had no wish to destroy his friendship with Sams—but he did have to insist that Sams leave. "We'll discuss this another time," he had told him. "When you can manage to get a grip on yourself."

He was hurt, deeply hurt, to see this side of his friend. Did Sams lie to protect his manhood because Eleanor had rejected him? Or was he acting out of jealousy over Tanner's success both with Eleanor and the ranch?

The whole thing had put a dismal pall over everything: the ranch, the work, even his time with Eleanor had been strained when he came inside after Sams left. She asked why Sams had not come in and joined them. Tanner was sure Eleanor saw through the excuse made up for his friend's abrupt absence.

But now the time he spent with his horses gave him solace. One gelding, a little buckskin, showed exceptional promise. After checking the colt's teeth, Tanner estimated the animal's age to be about four years. But the small horse showed uncommon maturity and settledness.

So calmly and matter-of-factly did the buckskin take to the procedure that at the end of that first work session, Tanner found himself in the saddle, riding tight circles and neat figure eights on the colt.

"Why, you little pisser," he remarked, patting the stout neck. "I might just hang on to you. I'm going to need me some extra smart horses for working stock, and I might just as well ride the best."

The buckskin's ears rotated toward the man on its back. It stamped a hoof impatiently.

"You're right, pardner," Tanner said to the horse, grinning. "I got carried away for a minute. It's time to quit for the night. You're right about that." He looked at the clear but fading sky. It was going to be cold again this night. In addition to his feeding chores, he would have to lug in a supply of firewood from the rapidly diminishing pile by the back door. He thought, as he brushed the buckskin, that he would soon have to snake a few deadfalls close to the house and go to work with ax and bucksaw, laying in a fresh supply of fuel.

By the time the feeding was done, he barely had strength to move his legs toward the house. It had been a while since he had put in a day such as this, and this was just the start. If he was going to make it on this place, he would have to drive himself for many years to come. But, God, it felt good. Soon, he would have a beautiful new wife, later maybe a couple of kids. Eleanor was certainly young enough to bear him children. And as far as his own age, he was feeling younger and more alive every day.

He was mounting the back steps with an armload of wood when his eyes were drawn toward the distant knoll. The hairs on the back of his neck prickled. He could barely make out a rider on the rise of ground. Tanner watched, fascinated by this apparition.

He dropped the load of wood and walked swiftly to the barn. Within minutes he had saddled the Appaloosa, pulling the reluctant horse from its supper of hay and oats. He stopped at the house long enough to get his Winchester.

Because of the high banks of the creekbed between himself and the unknown horseman, Tanner was forced to approach the rider from an oblique angle, crossing the creek at a spot considerably to the right of his course. Once lined out on flat ground, he moved his horse into an easy lope and watched the immobile figure in the distance for signs of breaking and running.

He had not long to wait. Abruptly, the head of the horseman jerked around. Then horse and rider were swept from Tanner's view beyond the knoll.

Tanner put spurs to the Appaloosa, and the startled animal leaped forward. Few horses could outrun Jake on open ground, and his staying power had at times surprised even Tanner. The deciding factor now was the swiftly approaching darkness.

Crouched low in the saddle on the running horse, Tanner plotted a likely course the fleeing rider might take. A moment later, the Appaloosa topped the rise at a bound. Tanner hauled on the reins, bringing the horse to a stop. The rider was nowhere in sight, and the imagined course Tanner had mapped out stretched stark and empty northward.

In the stretch of ground ahead, occasional patches of brush dotted the darkening landscape, adding to the confusion. The Appaloosa danced impatiently while Tanner searched for movement, sound, anything to give him a hint as to the direction the rider may have taken. Off to the left a flicker of movement caught his eye, a briefest glimpse as the fleeing horse and rider disappeared again.

The Appaloosa was ready to run, and it hit full stride almost immediately. Tanner turned the horse loose, trusting it to find secure footing over the soft ground that was now only a frightening blur beneath the pounding hooves.

But the race was quickly proving hopeless. Tanner had only a general idea of the direction of the quarry, and therein lay his frustration, for the last tack the rider had taken was angling farther west and south, toward town, or the McIntosh ranch.

The wind whipped at the collar of his coat. Cheekbones and ears grew numb, and the freezing air caused tears to stream from his eyes.

Now the Appaloosa raced against the darkness; unless Tanner gained visual contact with them soon, it would be too late. Horse and rider would be swallowed up by the cold night.

The Appaloosa stumbled, caught itself, stumbled again, and went down, somersaulting, throwing Tanner onto the rough ground ahead.

Tanner lay for a moment, dazed. Gradually the blur of early-evening stars floating overhead drifted into focus. Next came awareness of the labored breathing of the horse, punctuated with grunts and wild thrashing.

A chilling dread gripped Tanner as he fought to pull himself together. He sat up slowly. He was in no great pain. Bruised, some scratches, but nothing broken. He looked around for the Appaloosa and found the animal ten paces behind him, lying on its side, thrashing as though a leg were broken.

"Aw, Jake," whispered Tanner, agonizing, fighting his way to his hands and knees and then lurching to his feet.

He approached the horse from the animal's backside, mindful of the slashing hooves, and placed a soothing hand on the sweating neck.

A glance at the animal's leg brought a smile of relief. During the somersaulting fall, a leather rein had somehow wrapped itself around the fetlock of the rear leg that now lay nearest the ground. The horse could not maneuver the leg under itself and thus was unable to rise. The big, white-rimmed eyes glared angrily, nostrils flared.

"Now, how in hell did you manage that?" Tanner laughed with relief and slapped the horse on the neck.

He talked the horse into lying calm and still, reached across the sweating flank, and freed the snarled rein from about the leg. The animal scrambled to its feet instantly, nostrils wide, blowing angrily. Jake shook himself and limped forward a few steps. Tanner watched, anxious for any sign of a serious injury. There would be some soreness in the morning for both of them, he concluded, but they both fared better than they had a right to expect after a fall such as that.

He righted the twisted saddle, tightened the cinch, and adjusted the rifle in the scabbard. And then he crawled painfully into the saddle.

There was no point thinking about renewing the chase, for it was now full dark. In the morning, perhaps, he would try to locate some tracks, but if the rider had continued his threatened course toward town, that, too, would be well-nigh useless.

It had been in his plans to ride into town the following morning for supplies, and he resolved, as he and the Appaloosa picked their painful way home, that he would drop by the sheriff's and mention this rider whose two visits had been far from sociable.

CHAPTER 12

TROY Sams nudged the bay gelding with his spurs. His idea was to hurry past the ranch house before old Jess Grant saw him.

It was no good. The boss sat upon his crude wooden porch, whiskey in hand, scowling as Sams rode past.

"Hell with 'im," Sams muttered. "He told me I could go." Grudgingly, though, the lanky rider was loath to admit to himself.

Aw well, he concluded, it was worth the displeasure of the boss to see Carrie. She had beckoned, *and to her side he must fly.* He grinned, kicked the horse, and waved at Grant.

"See ya this evening, Mr. Grant," he called to his unresponsive employer. "An' thanks again." And he added under his breath, "Yeah. Thanks, you ol' fart."

He turned his horse's head north, leaving Crater Road, which circled Sweetwater on the west side, and headed cross country toward the Farley ranch.

He rode swiftly, for he was hungry, and the anticipation of a plate of Carrie's cold fried chicken and a bellyful of Mr. Farley's fine home-brewed beer was worth the drudgery of watching Carrie one more time put that infernal stallion through its paces.

He was to be witness to the first ride, she had promised last evening. She said the stallion had accepted the first saddling as calmly as though it were an everyday occurrence.

Well, Sams thought grimly, getting a saddle on the horse was one thing. Having someone sitting in that saddle was an entirely different matter. And that was far too dangerous for Carrie, no matter what she might think.

He intended to sweet-talk, cajole, argue, or threaten Carrie into letting him be the first to ride the horse. She was so goddamn stubborn. Reminded him a bit of Tanner.

He smarted at the thought. Tanner.

Well, he'd probably shot that friendship all to hell. Tellin' him all about Eleanor. Damn! Why, in God's name, hadn't he kept his big mouth shut?

His thoughts broke off when he looked up to find a large white-tail buck regarding him from a willow stand off to his right.

"Ah-ha," Sams said softly, and pulled the bay to a stand. Now, if he could nail that big fella and take him back to Jess Grant as a peace offering, he might just be able to smooth some ruffled feathers. He chuckled. *Might even get myself an extra day off,* he mused, pulling his Winchester from the saddle boot.

The buck, with a magnificent full rack indicating years of survival sense, began walking cautiously from the willows toward the grove of pine and spruce trees just ahead on the trail.

Sams nudged the bay forward. "Now, now. Let's not be shy," he urged the wary deer, moving in earnest toward the cover of the trees. The buck made a break for it, leaping twenty feet down the slope, landing like a steel spring at the very edge of the grove.

Sams raised the rifle and snapped off one quick shot before the deer's next bound cleared a large laurel bush and the animal disappeared from view.

"I'll be goddamned!" cursed Troy, spurring the bay.

He reached the edge of the trees in time to see the buck's white tail, like a retreating banner, disappear into the gloom of the trees.

He pulled the bay to a walk and began threading his careful way through the grove. He found the way strewn with limbs and tangles that could easily bring down a horse—break a leg, or worse.

Sams had come this way before. It was a bit shorter, cutting perhaps a quarter-mile from the trip to the Farley ranch. Moreover, in the grove's exact center there was a small, idyllic clearing with a stream and sweet grass. It was here he figured the buck might go. It was worth a look-see, anyway.

The woods were quiet. From somewhere ahead a magpie scolded, perhaps at the buck. The ground was soft and mushy from recently melted snow, and the bay's steps were soundless. Troy found it pleasant among the pine trees, shielded from the cold breeze he had faced out on the flats.

In the silence, and with the gentle motion of the horse, he grew contemplative, weighing once more his last words with Tanner, measuring the rift that now lay between them.

When he reached the clearing, his mind was far removed from the buck, so that when he came upon the animal, standing ankle-deep in the stream, Sams was jolted.

The buck shook its magnificent rack, gave Sams one last pained look, and then bounded across the stream and disappeared into the trees.

"Sonofabitch!" Sams jacked a shell into the chamber of his rifle, futiley scanned the trees for the buck's disappearing hindquarters, and then jammed the weapon back into the scabbard. "Another day, you bastard," he called after the deer, but he was smiling. The buck had beat him fair and square.

He should have noticed the dark horse and rider first off. He probably would have, had it not been for the buck. This was the second time within minutes he had been caught by surprise. Instinctively, he reached for the rifle.

He never heard the shot. The force of the slug slammed his head back, sent his hat flying, and carried him careening over backward, knocked from the saddle.

The heavy report of the rifle rocketed among the pines, lending wings to the flying hooves of the buck, now racing through the woods a quarter-mile from the clearing.

In Sheriff Reynolds's office, Tanner placed his empty cup on the desk, and asked, "Making any headway on the Bridges killing?"

Reynolds shook his head. "No, I ain't got a damn thing. Except he was shot in the head close, probably by someone he knew."

"I don't know what it's worth, Loyal, but I've been seeing a strange rider out a ways. I saw him yesterday for the second time and gave him a chase. I lost him in the dark. It's a weird thing. Kind of get the feeling he's been eying me, keeping tabs on me, of sorts."

"Get close enough to get a look?" Reynolds's face betrayed cautious interest. He sucked reflectively on one corner of his mustache.

Tanner shook his head. "Not from a quarter-mile away I didn't. Somebody dressed in dark clothes. The horse was brown, maybe black—and very fast. That horse of mine can run, but in a short race he wouldn't have stood a chance."

Reynolds pushed himself upright. "Now, you listen to me. If you happen on this mysterious gent again, you do your damnedest to run his ass into the ground. Maybe he has something to do with Bridges, maybe not. But I got a real need to confer with the bastard, all the same."

Tanner was stepping out on the sidewalk when Reynolds's final words caught up with him. "An' be real careful, Lee. I don't want to be findin' you with a slug between your eyes."

Carrie Farley tied the stallion to a fence rail, placed a saddle pad on its back, and settled the saddle gently into place. She took extreme care that the stirrups and the cinch did not suddenly drop and slap the animal's sides. Through all this the colt merely eyed her curiously.

She let it wear the saddle while she went about the rest of her chores. When the sun was overhead, she stripped the saddle off, leaving it handy for that first ride later, and groomed and brushed the horse and gave it a small portion of grain before returning to the house to prepare lunch for herself and Sams.

Carrie was pleased with herself. She felt she had already undone the harm Gentry had inflicted on the horse. She had not forgotten Tanner's promise to look in on her, and she felt sure he would be impressed with her progress.

When the meal was ready, she set places for the two of them at the kitchen table and then took a seat on the front steps to await Troy's arrival. Her father, she knew, would not return until late afternoon. A few odd head of cattle had disappeared from the range north, and he had ridden to Fort Granger to report the matter. In his estimation it had been the work of a small band of Utes, strayed from the reservation, scavenging off the land whatever loose livestock they could find. Not a serious matter yet, but one that needed attention.

She sat with her arms wrapped about her knees, looking out across the empty land. The countryside was strangely silent. No breeze for the moment. Birds were stilled. It was as though the land waited for a storm. Carrie checked the cloudless horizon.

About one o'clock, she grew impatient. At one-thirty, thoroughly put out, Carrie saddled her horse, a small-boned dun mare, and rode out of the ranch yard, heading southeast, the direction from which Sams would come.

She was not worried, only irritated. He accepted the term *promptness* with the same casual attitude he accepted everything else.

In her saddlebags she had packed their lunch, cold fried chicken and hard-baked, black rye bread, a meal she knew to be among his favorites.

When she met up with him, they could stop, build a fire, and make coffee and eat their lunch right there.

She shivered. The chill breeze had reawakened, and now pushed icily at her back.

Twenty minutes from the ranch yard, Carrie dropped into

a wooded arroyo, channeling down into the grove of close-grown pines.

At the lip of the cut, the dun mare locked its forelegs, sat down upon its haunches, and, amid an avalanche of gravel and dirt, slid its way to the bottom.

Carrie reached forward and patted the little animal on its arched, proud neck, nudging it along the obscure animal trail leading through the grove.

A shot, like the snapping of a large tree branch, filled the matted grove about her.

Very close. Carrie jumped. The mare flinched and stopped dead in its tracks, ears laid back flat against its head, shoulders hunched. Carrie reached forward and placed a soothing hand on the animal's neck, the while looking about uncertainly.

A few minutes later, another shot sounded. This time, listening close, she determined the sound as coming from just ahead, perhaps on the far side of the basin.

A branch snapped, off to her left. A buck dashed off, moving fast, so fast she had time only to turn her head before it had disappeared among the trees.

She smiled and started the mare forward. Sams must have made a stab at bringing down some venison. She would be sure to comment upon his marksmanship, she promised.

Suddenly, another figure passed through the brush to her right, larger and heavier than the buck. An elk maybe, or someone on horseback.

"Troy?" she called uncertainly. Why was he moving rapidly off in the wrong direction—the buck had gone the other way. "Troy?"

Silence was her answer. No more movement. No sound. Nothing.

Carrie had the uncomfortable feeling she was being watched. And she was sure it wasn't Troy.

She reached for her saddle scabbard and cursed. Like a fool, she had left her rifle at the ranch. She eased forward and started toward the Jess Grant ranch; surely she would run into Sams.

She followed the game trail downward toward a dish-shaped clearing. As she approached, she spotted tracks. They belonged to the bay Sams rode. The animal was a slew-foot, its tracks distinctive and easy to spot.

She followed the tracks through the bushes into the clearing and pulled the dun mare to a stand. Her eyes grew wide in horror.

The body lay where it had fallen.

As Tanner rode along the narrow wagon road toward the Farley place, his thoughts were plagued by the unknown rider. The horseman had posed no actual threat to Tanner, like a passing storm cloud that threatens but gives up no rain.

Still, there was something hauntingly familiar in that lonesome figure. Maybe it was that familiarity that bred his sudden unrest. He raked over his past, dredging up names and faces, but none would sift down to anything solid. He had no real enemies he could think of—surely none that would approach him skulking or circling around like a hungry buzzard.

At the ranch, a young cowhand told him, "Hell, you should've bumped right into her. She left about a half hour ago. Reckon she lit out lookin' fer that Troy guy. He was s'posed to be out this afternoon but ain't shown up so far."

Tanner detected a wistful note in the young man's tone. Another one smitten, he thought with a bemused smile. Watch out, Troy.

He picked up the fresh hoofprints a short way from the ranch and settled into an easy lope, following the trail across the spongy grassland.

After a while, he heard the faint report of muffled gunfire. One shot. Two. More? He couldn't be sure.

When he reached the pine grove, all senses were alert, eyes

and ears tuned for any slight movement or sound. He pulled Jake to a walk and loosened the leather thong from the hammer of his six-gun.

The tracks he had been following became obscured in the thick needles and brush at the base of the pines. He moved now by instinct rather than design, easing his way, fighting back the urge for haste. If someone had designs for setting a trap, he could ask for no better cover than the thick grove with all its deluding shadows, its swirls and eddies of light and dark.

Tanner worked his way down the path, inclining toward the floor of the gully, searching as he went for signs of a recent body passing. Carrie's path had to lie in this direction. He spotted only an occasional scuff mark where the mat of brown rotting needles was momentarily scraped aside.

From below came the sudden furious sound of a heavy animal passing through the brush.

Tanner pulled up Jake and drew his six-gun. Things were getting just a little too goddamn spooky in these woods for his taste.

A horse bearing an empty saddle came lunging up the path. It was Carrie's small dun mare. When the horse encountered Tanner astride Jake, it slowed not at all, bumping past the larger horse, fighting its way upward toward open ground and some wide-open running room. It was clear to Tanner that the animal had been frightened by something behind it.

He waited his horse until the mare had disappeared and the sound of its passing had faded, and then, gun in hand, he nudged Jake forward and downward.

It had to have been Carrie's horse. Tanner knew the bay Sams rode.

Tanner tapped Jake's flanks with his spurs and set the powerful horse crashing through tall, thick brush and into the clearing beyond.

His eyes fell first upon the horse, Troy's bay. It lay thrashing upon the ground. Its legs churned weakly. Blood and red foam issued from a wound in its chest.

Tanner rode slowly, pistol in hand, past the horse to the body of his friend. A glance told him it was hopeless. The blood beneath Troy's head had thickened to a red, coagulated mass.

"Ah, Troy. You poor old son of a bitch," he muttered in a hurting whisper.

He glanced quickly about and saw Carrie lying partially submerged in the stream nearby.

He dropped from the horse and waded the stream. He knelt in the shallow water where Carrie's upper torso rested on the bank.

"Carrie, not you too," he murmured. He took Carrie's hand and found it warm, and hope surged through him. Quickly he removed his hat and placed an ear to her chest. At least she was still alive.

Tanner looked her over for bullet wounds and found none. A large, bluish lump rose on her forehead, and her right forearm was twisted at a crazy angle, surely broken. She was badly hurt, but she would live—he was sure of it.

His worry now was getting her home. There was nothing to be done for Troy. He would have to send the sheriff and some men out from town, along with a wagon.

A low nicker from Sams's downed horse prompted Tanner into movement. He glanced about, searching the area for Carrie's horse, and then recalled the animal had bolted past him on the trail. It didn't matter. She would have to be held on a horse anyway.

He worked her carefully onto dry ground, anxious that he not disturb the injured arm too much.

Tanner walked over to the dying horse, patted its sweating neck reassuringly, and then shot it in the head. There was an almost grateful sigh from the bay, and then it was still.

It was nearly dark when Tanner reached the Farley ranch with Carrie. Timmy Rawlins, the young cowhand Tanner had talked to earlier, helped carry the injured girl into the house and lay her on a bed. This was just accomplished when Andy Farley, confused and questioning, appeared in the doorway.

"What in the hell?" he asked, rushing to his daughter's bedside.

"I'll explain everything," Tanner said to Farley. Then he turned to Rawlins. "Right now, you've got to get into town and get the doctor and the sheriff."

Rawlins looked at Tanner, and then at the unconscious, bruised girl on the bed. He nodded and ran out.

Tanner lit a lamp on a stand by the bed. Then he and Farley took turns wringing out rags in cold water, bathing Carrie's face and hands, and placing compresses on her bruised forehead.

CHAPTER 13

THE violent death of his friend had struck Tanner deeply. He wandered about for days, doing chores, working the young horses, doing all the mechanical things of his existence that had to be done, yet feeling none of the hope or exhilaration that had spurred him on only a few days earlier. His thoughts centered on the murder—the ugliness and, most of all, the senselessness of it. Along with the anger, he was troubled by the memory of how harshly he and Sams had last parted company.

When Carrie was able to hold down her end of a lucid conversation and to deal with the sheriff's questions, she had been able to contribute little to the picture. She had heard shots, discovered Troy, had herself been run down from behind by someone on a horse. That was all she could remember.

Doctor Brennan had set her broken arm, and he said she would recover completely from the head wound. But recovering from the shock of Troy Sams's death would be another matter.

At the doctor's suggestion, Andy Farley had arranged for Angus McIntosh's wife to come and stay with Carrie until she improved enough to manage on her own.

Every day or so, Tanner made an effort to ride over and check on things. Rawlins and Farley's two older hands put in extra hours, handling Carrie's chores around the ranch. No one really needed Tanner, but his presence always seemed to brighten Carrie's mood a little, although she was still grief-stricken over Troy's death.

It was during these visits that he began to appreciate the

girl's resilience and her sense of humor. Her ability to laugh returned first. More often than not, after a session of exchanging barbs with the girl, it was Tanner who rode away with spirits lifted.

During the days following Sams's death, Eleanor Tate was suffering too. Between Tanner's work and his visits to the Farley ranch, he spent little time with her. On occasions when they could be together, he seemed tired and withdrawn. She felt angry and resentful that, as her wedding day approached—scarcely six weeks away now—her man spent less and less time with her.

She resented anyone and anything that took attention away from her. She was sick of hearing about his damn horses. She was sick of hearing about this mysterious killer no one could catch. And she was especially sick of hearing him speak of Carrie Farley. He was neglecting his fiancée so that he might ride over and hold that wretch's hand.

CHAPTER 14

SATURDAY afternoon, one week after the killing, Tanner was in the round pen working a recently gelded colt when Eleanor rode up. At the sight of Eleanor's mare across the fence, the colt arched its neck and gave a startled side jump, nearly unseating Tanner. The violent lurch caused Tanner's back to twist at a painful angle.

Tanner pulled the horse into a tight circle and brought it under control. He directed a cool glance at the waiting Eleanor and stepped from the saddle. This day wasn't going right at all, and he was in no mood to fight either a rank horse or a woman bearing the cloudy looks of the blond facing him across the fence.

Eleanor sensed his mood, and her manner changed instantly. A warm smile spread across her lips, and her eyes brightened invitingly.

Tanner climbed up and seated himself on the top rail of the fence.

"I was beginning to think you had left the country," she said pleasantly enough. "You're finding more pleasure in the company of these damn horses than spending time with me."

Tanner smiled back. Though he used it himself all too often, he found profanity always sounded strange coming from her lips.

"I know what to expect from a bronc. A woman's a little different story. I saw you ride in with that sour look on your face, and I figured I was in for some rough weather."

"I'm concerned about you," she answered seriously. "That's what that look meant. Don't misread it." Her gaze was steady.

His answering stare was just as firm. "All right. Now, what brings you out this way? You don't expect me to stop my work and entertain you?"

"That's exactly what I want, mister. I haven't spent more than twenty minutes with you in the last two weeks." She dropped from the saddle with a short bounce. "Come down off that fence, cowboy, and show me some affection."

He dropped with a dusty jolt, and she reached up and slipped her arms around his neck. After a prolonged kiss, they moved off toward the house, arm in arm.

Inside, Tanner added a few sticks to the smoldering breakfast fire and set a fresh pot of coffee on to brew. While they waited, they walked from room to room, talking about their future home.

"I never dreamed it would turn out this nice," she said, breathlessly. "To tell you the truth, darling, I was not looking forward to leaving Daddy's big old barn of a house and moving into a run-down farmhouse with a new coat of paint and fresh wallpaper. But this is wonderful. I mean it."

Though he was around it every day, Tanner himself was impressed. It had turned out quite nice. A bit too fancy for a single man living alone, but nice enough that a delicate woman could feel comfortable entertaining her friends.

He reached out and touched the textured wallpaper in the front room. The small but tasteful chandelier sparkled overhead. The floor was polished. The decorating ideas were Eleanor's. She had personally overseen the selection of every piece of furniture.

Over coffee in the kitchen, their conversation dwindled and then died altogether. For a time each seemed lost in thought.

Finally he asked, "Are you getting anxious?"

She looked up from her cup and smiled. "Of course. Really, it hasn't been that long, but it seems like we've been waiting forever."

"The time's been flying for me," said Tanner. "I'm so damn busy, I've been meeting myself coming back."

"That's the hard part," she said with a sad smile. "I don't have a lot left to do now but wait to see you. And you're so occupied you probably don't even think of me until you see me ride up." Her smile turned reproachful.

"Now, that just isn't so." He reached across the table and took her hand. "Whatever I'm doing, no matter where I'm at, I always take you with me."

She patted his hand like an indulgent child. "That's sweet. I have an idea—why don't you get back to work, while I stick around and throw you together some supper."

Tanner appeared uneasy. "Eleanor, that sounds nice, dinner and everything. But I've got something else I got to see to." He hastened to explain. "I've been helping out at the Farley place whenever I can. Right now they're dropping pipe for the new windmill. I said I'd ride over later and give them a hand. Mrs. McIntosh usually has a plate of something set back for me when I'm over there," he finished lamely.

Two cold blue eyes met his. She was silent for several moments, continuing the while to stare at him, through him.

Finally she asked, "What the hell are you trying to do?" It seemed that the very act of speaking ignited her anger. Her cheeks flamed and her nostrils widened.

"I'm trying to be a good neighbor," he answered stiffly. "The Farleys are my friends." He thought, she has no right to be doing this. "If the situation were reversed, they would be doing exactly the same thing for me."

"I doubt that!" she answered flatly. "You spend so much time over there because you want to see Carrie!"

With an effort Tanner controlled himself. "Eleanor, you're not thinking straight. I feel an obligation to help her. And that's all. Don't put a meaning on it that isn't there."

She was not ready to be placated. "Lee, others can look in on her and others can help her. For God's sake! She's got her father! You've done enough!" Angry tears welled up in her eyes and splashed down her cheeks. "You are supposed to be getting things ready for our marriage. Or have you forgotten about that?"

"I haven't forgotten," he answered wearily. "We agreed I'd get this first bunch of horses broke and sold to the Army before the wedding. I'm almost there now."

"I'm surprised you've been able to accomplish anything, as much time as you've spent with her."

Tanner's jaw dropped. "Eleanor, listen to yourself!" he exclaimed. "You can't really believe anything like that!"

"What am I supposed to believe?" she cried, striking the tabletop with her small hand. "When was the last time you were out to the ranch to spend any time with me? When was the last time we had dinner in town or went for a ride together?"

Tanner shook his head sadly and looked down into his coffee cup. "If I've been neglecting you, hon, I'm sorry. I really am. But I swear there is nothing between Carrie and me."

She glared at him and stood up. "I've got to go," she said, and pushed past him. She threw open the back door and stormed down the wooden steps.

He followed after and tried to help her mount, but she struck his hands away.

He reached around and grabbed the bridle of the mare. "This is stupid, Eleanor. Get down off that horse. Let's walk a spell and work this thing out."

She jerked the reins, pulling the mare's head around. "Go to hell! That is, if you can spare the time away from Carrie!"

She jammed her spurs into the frightened mare, and the horse jumped forward. Tanner watched with aching heart until she disappeared.

CHAPTER 15

EARLY on a Sunday afternoon, Billy Tate emerged from the ranch house and directed his steps toward the stable. As he neared the door, he heard stamping hooves and sounds of scuffling about.

He swung the door wide, exposing Eleanor, who stood before a stall, quirt in her upraised hand, wisps of blond hair flying about her red, angry face. In the stall, angry eyes flashed back. Savage hooves dug at the clay floor.

Billy's mouth dropped open. "Dad'll kill you if he catches you beatin' on that horse!"

"To hell with him!" she spat. "And to hell with you!" She flung the quirt against the wall and stormed out, slamming the stable door behind her.

Billy stood aghast. He had seen his sister's outbursts before. And he had seen her vent her anger on servants and animals. But even Eleanor would not be exempt from the wrath of John Tate if anything happened to Venus. John Tate was proud of his many possessions: his leather-bound classics, his collection of Civil War weapons, and his wine cellar all held place in a special section of his heart. But next to Eleanor, this little Thoroughbred filly was Tate's crowning jewel. He had bought Venus only last year for a huge sum, and the horse was to be the beginning for a great strain of racing thoroughbreds.

As for Billy, he was truly in awe of the filly. Venus was the most beautiful horse he had ever seen. Its long, beautiful head with wide-set, intelligent eyes seemed to float above the superbly muscled neck. He particularly admired the animal's coat: a deep, deep red coat, ready to turn black, glittering like moonlight on a night river.

He reached quickly into the stall and caught the filly by its leather halter.

He whistled softly. A raw welt had spread across the horse's graceful neck.

"If the old man sees that," he mused aloud, "hell's to pay."

Hell would pay, too, if the old man were aware that Billy was also riding the filly as frequently as he desired. Eleanor, because of her light weight and her superb horsemanship, was the only one permitted to exercise the horse.

Billy made sure, each time he rode Venus, his father was not on the ranch and would not soon return.

To Billy, riding this horse was worth the risks. Being astride its long-legged grace made him somehow superior to the rest of the world, much as when he strapped the ever-present six-gun into place. He would gladly have given everything he possessed to own this one horse.

The rest of the horses he treated with disdain. In his young lifetime, he had ridden one horse to death and ruined several others. But this horse was special. He fingered the welt and cursed Eleanor. Well, if push came to shove, he just might have to tell the old man about this himself. Serve her right.

The stable door swung wide, and Eleanor stormed in. She had changed her dress and was now wearing riding pants. She gave Billy one withering glance and walked past him to the empty stall that served as a tack room.

Billy folded his arms across his narrow chest and observed his sister. If there was one thing he enjoyed, it was baiting Eleanor. The more angry she became, the more fun it was for him. Today, he could tell, she was already far along. He grinned.

He watched lazily as Eleanor hooked a line onto the filly's halter, led it from the stall, and began saddling the animal.

"And just what might Daddy's little girl be up to today?"

"Don't start with me, Billy!" Her eyes flashed. She jerked on the leather cinch, startling the filly, which tried to sidestep away from the commotion. The woman slapped the horse on the neck so hard that it caused her hand to sting. She knotted an angry fist.

Billy chuckled. "Daddy won't like it—you hittin' his horse that way."

"I don't give a damn what Daddy likes! And I told you to shut up!" She slapped the mare again, and this time the animal reared, held in check only by the lead line cinched tight through an iron ring implanted in one of the roof supports.

Billy jumped, dodged to one side, and stood there blinking. He watched Eleanor reach for the lead, pull the filly's head down, and bring the animal under control. Billy's plans about tormenting his sister had changed abruptly. She was too hot to fool with just now.

"Easy, sis," he implored. "Something's botherin' you, but it ain't worth gettin' us both killed over."

"What did I tell—"

"Hold on! Hold on!" he urged. "I'm not going to pester you. I can see you ain't in the mood for fun right now."

"You're damn right I'm not!" She went back to outfitting the filly.

"Come to think of it," he said after a few moments of watching her fight stubborn buckles and tangled reins, "you seemed out of sorts when you came home from . . . Tanner's yesterday." There was the silent beat of a second or two, and then his eyes lit up unbidden, triumphant.

"You had a fight!" he crowed. "Lord, have mercy. The couple has been torn asunder!"

Eleanor, face flushed with fury, fists clinched into hard little knots, took a threatening step toward Billy.

"Okay, okay." He laughed, holding up his hands and taking a step backward. "I didn't mean to laugh, really." With an effort he brought himself under control and assumed as best he could a sympathetic face. He even ventured to move close to her and place a comforting hand on her shoulder, which she struck away sharply.

"Calm down," he urged, now fully under control. A breakup of the marriage plans would take care of all his worries concerning his future and the future of the ranch.

"Okay, you and Tanner had a fight," he said, trying to sound offhand, yet inviting confidence. This was new ground for Billy. Diplomacy and manipulation were concepts rather foreign to him. "Listen, ol' gal, I know you're not in the mood, so I'm not going to ask you a lot of ques—"

"Just stay out of it," she snapped, turning back to the horse. And then, over her shoulder, "Yes. We had a fight. Happy?"

He pondered a moment, seeming to give the matter sober consideration, and then said, "I'm sorry, sis. Really I am."

"I'll just bet," she snorted. She grabbed a stirrup and swung into the saddle. "Listen, Billy." She held the dancing, nervous horse in check. "Keep your mouth shut and keep all your opinions to yourself. If you'll just do that much, I'll be eternally grateful." She wheeled the horse around. Spurs flashed, and she was gone through the open stable doors.

Billy stood looking after her, smiling a little, rocking gently back and forth on the balls of his feet, his old, scuffed boots forgotten.

CHAPTER 16

TANNER folded the telegram and stuffed it in his coat pocket. He had mixed feelings about the contents. The Army at Fort Blaine had jumped at the prospect of buying the fifteen ready-to-ride mounts. The one catch, the quartermaster had wired, was the Army's budget. Funds to pay for the new mounts would not be available for another sixty days.

Tanner grimaced. His first payment to the bank was due in less than a month. Eight hundred dollars was the amount required. Although John Tate had assured him repeatedly that the bank would be lenient and understanding until Tanner was on his feet, Tanner didn't want to start the thing out this way, late on his first payment.

Of course, there was still his own money in the bank, the nearly two thousand dollars he had ridden in with. He needed to reflect only a moment to decide. That is what he'd do—make his bank payment out of that sum, and then replace it when the Army came through.

He felt a little better now. As a matter of fact, he felt pretty damn good. Better than he thought he ever could after his argument with Eleanor last week. He took the note from his pocket, the one a Tate ranch hand had delivered last evening.

In the note, Eleanor had said she was sorry about their argument and had invited him to dinner at the ranch Monday evening.

For Tanner, the note was an answer to his prayers. He had spent a miserable week; aside from working, he scarcely ventured from the house. He deeply regretted his own well-meant but ill-advised actions and the rest of the circumstances that had joined forces to make him appear fickle and as though he were taking Eleanor for granted. He had hoped desperately the storm would blow over, and yesterday he was even considering a ride over to the Tate ranch. But that's when Jenks brought the note.

Tanner mounted the Appaloosa and started out of town at a lope. It was just past noon, and he still had much to do before dinner at the Tate's.

As he rode past the sheriff's office, Reynolds hailed him.

"Hold up there, Tanner."

Tanner pulled up and waited as Reynolds, puffing, lumbered from the boardwalk out to the center of the street.

"You in such a all-fired hurry you can't stop an' have a cup?"

"Got better things to do," Tanner answered. "Like working. You ought to give it a try."

"An' spoil a clean record? Not on your life."

He placed a hand on the Appaloosa's neck and leaned for support, as though the horse alone kept him from falling on his face in the street.

"I do have one little bit of news I want you to chew on." Reynolds directed a jet of tobacco juice into the dirt. "I was out to that gully where you found Sams. Been out there a couple of times—lookin' around, tryin' to sniff out some little thing to hang a hunch on. An', by damn, I found me some hoofprints." He spat again and wiped his lips and mustache with the heel of his hand.

"Now, down in the gully the ground was all mussed up. We both know that. There had been at least four horses down there. So's I got to checkin' up on that hillside, in among the trees, an' I found a half-dozen good clear prints. There was a little spot there 'twas pretty clear—no leaves or brush. The prints showed up plain as day."

"You think it might be the killer's horse?" Tanner asked.

"I stood my own horse in that same spot. It would give me clear view into the gully—fifteen, twenty yards at most."

"Sounds like it might fit, all right. Anything unusual about the horse? Think you could identify it from the prints?"

Reynolds's expression clouded. "Not for sure. Nothing that would stand up, anyways. 'Bout all I can say for sure is it was a small horse, or one with unusually small hooves."

Tanner thought for a moment. It was his unconscious habit to notice most horses he saw. He seldom forgot the particulars of build, conformation, gait.

"Don't ring a bell, Sheriff. You wouldn't happen to know the color of its eyes, would you? It would help a lot." He grinned into the sheriff's upturned face.

Reynolds spat. "Very funny. Keep an eye out, will you? Considering your business, you see more horses than most."

"Count on it." He started to ride off, but then hesitated. "Do me a favor too. Keep an eye on Carrie for a while. I've been riding out there a little too often, and I've been falling behind in my own work. Miz McIntosh went on home, and Farley's busy with the operation. She still needs a look-see every now and then."

"I can do that," he said with an emphatic nod. "Be glad to. Mighty sweet little gal. My heart breaks for her." He wiped his chin, waved a hand, and turned to slog back to his office.

Tanner worked in the round pen until nearly four o'clock, at which time he decided to knock off early so he would have time to clean up before heading over to the Tate ranch. An hour later, bathed and shaved and in his best clothes, he mounted the Appaloosa and struck out on the now very familiar path.

As he left the low, rolling hills of his own land and crossed over to the slightly more level Tate property, he felt a pang of nervousness, almost fear. So much was riding on this meeting with Eleanor.

All day long Sunday, he had lived with the unnerving prospect that he might be losing her. And over something so ridiculous as her jealousy of Carrie. Of course, Carrie was attractive, and she was a good, comfortable person to be with. But he loved Eleanor, and somehow he must make Eleanor realize it. She had nothing to fear from Carrie or any other woman.

What a fool he had been. Sure, Carrie needed help. But, as Eleanor had pointed out, there were plenty of others to lend a hand. Look how quick the sheriff was to agree to help. And there was Carrie's own father. Sure, Farley was busy with his work this time of year, but not too busy to tend to his daughter!

I should've been more listening to my own woman's needs and feelings, he lashed himself. Pray to God I can straighten this thing out. I *will* straighten out the whole damn mess, he resolved. And I'll do it tonight.

It was nearly dusk when he sighted the lights of the ranch and urged the Appaloosa to quicken its pace.

He heard the hoofbeats first, and he cocked his head to one side. Because of the gloom, he could not at first tell from which direction the sound came. One rider. Moving fast.

The hairs on the back of his neck rose, and a chill fingered his spine.

He pulled to a stop and twisted in the saddle, searching the darkening landscape for movement. At first it was only a blur, a fleet shadow cast by moving clouds and a toenail of a moon. He checked it with his peripheral vision. It was still there. It was solid, not merely a shadow. And it was coming fast.

The beats grew stronger, and the flying form took on shape and dark substance.

Tanner spun the Appaloosa. It struck him suddenly that the horse and rider were bearing directly down upon him. But it was, he realized, only an illusion caused by the ghostly light. The flight of the running horse was at an angle that would intersect Tanner's path a good hundred yards ahead, and that would carry the horse and rider to the doorstep of the Tate ranch house.

Tanner watched as the horse whipped past, moving at an incredible speed.

He jammed with his spurs, and the Appaloosa shot ahead. But after only a few strides, Tanner knew that the chase was hopeless. The only way he could hope to catch up with the flying horse was if it fell and broke a leg. He was able to keep it in sight, only long enough to confirm that it was indeed heading for the ranch.

The drumming of the hoofbeats faded, and the horse and rider were swallowed into the blackness.

Tanner slowed his horse to a walk and approached the ranch warily. As his eyes searched among the shadows of the outbuildings, he loosened his gun in its holster and pulled his coat flap away to allow quick access.

From the open stable door the soft yellow glow of a coal oil lantern flickered into life.

Tanner dismounted and tied his horse at the hitch rack closest to the house and then made his way softly on foot to the stable.

It struck him nearly as a revelation to see at last, within the lighted stable, the horse he had almost convinced himself did not exist.

He walked boldly, right hand hanging free and close to his gun.

If the horse belonged on the ranch, how had he missed seeing it? In all his trips to the Tate ranch, could it be only chance that had seen to it their paths, his and the dark horse's, had not crossed.

The mystery and questions faded. He stood in the open doorway, gaping in openmouthed worship of one of the finest horses he had ever laid eyes on. The yellow light from the lamp sent shivers of gold across the silky coat. The head, the pert, small ears, the placement of the eyes, and the set of the magnificent neck made the horse more a statue carved from flawless marble than a living, breathing creature.

The filly was tied by a lead rope to a support beam. It

stepped about nervously, rolling its large, dark eyes at Tanner. It nickered shrilly, and the sound reverberated among the stable beams.

There was movement beyond the filly. A dark form materialized from the shadows of a stall and spoke. "Just what the hell are you looking for?"

Tanner found himself looking into the surprised and angry face of Billy Tate. He was quick to notice Billy was not armed. Tanner eased his right hand forward, away from his own gun.

"You got no business in here. Strangers ain't allowed around the horses. 'Specially this one." A cynical smile flickered. "An' from what sis tells me, you're the next best thing to bein' a stranger right now."

Tanner moved slowly forward, keeping his motion loose and casual. "Fine animal," he said. "Why don't I believe this is your horse?"

Billy's eyes locked menacingly with Tanner's across the rump of the filly. "Meanin' what?"

"Meaning nothing. Except I can't see John Tate sinking a bunch of money into a horse this fine just so his spoiled kid could go tearing around the countryside in the dark. You know how easy it would be to break a leg out there, moving out the way you were?"

Tanner detected alarm in Billy's eyes.

"It's none of your business." Billy turned away and began rubbing down the sweating horse with some burlap. "Horse needs exercisin', don't it?"

"Is that what you were doing over at my place that evening?"

"I don't know what the hell you're talkin' about." Billy cast a nervous glance toward the open door. "I never been over at your place. Least not since you moved in."

"That's funny." Tanner's tone was disbelieving. "I could've sworn I've seen the tail end of that horse before."

Billy threw the wet burlap across a stall door and turned to confront Tanner.

"I ain't interested in what you thought you saw." He walked past Tanner, looked outside quickly, and then closed the stable door.

"Here's the truth, Tanner." There was a grudging but nearly conciliatory note in the young man's voice. "All right. I've been ridin' her. Once, twice a week. But I ain't been over at your place. An' neither has this horse."

Tanner considered Billy's nervousness, the cautious glances over his shoulder at the closed stable door.

"You've been taking her out behind your father's back."

Billy paused a moment, then nodded. "Damn horse is worth more to him than me," he grumbled. "Dad bought her to start a string for racin'. Got his eye on a stallion right now. Big-time money winner."

"And naturally, you just had to take her out to see what she could do—Daddy or no."

"It wasn't like that!" Billy declared. "You never been on a horse like that, Tanner. She damn near flys. I tell you, it's the best damn feelin'!"

"I'll have to give you that much," agreed Tanner, running his eyes over the horse's sleek lines. "She is built for speed."

"You're damn right. Just look at that chest—all that lung space. Slender legs and those small hooves." Billy rambled on. He seemed to have forgotten Tanner's presence. "See how her neck flows into those shoulders and withers? She's balanced perfect, I tell you!"

Tanner agreed. He turned and started for the door.

"Tanner!" Billy's voice was urgent. "Are you going to tell him?" The young man's face was a humorous mixture of defiance and fear. "He'll crucify me if he finds out."

Tanner paused to consider. He honestly would rather not say anything to John Tate. But, then again, if something happened and John Tate ever got wind that Tanner knew that Billy was riding the animal . . .

But there were other matters to consider. Could this still somehow be the horse the sheriff was looking for?

He recalled Billy's ruthlessness with a six-gun, his temper. But why would he kill Sams? It just didn't add up, at least not yet.

Tanner frowned and shook his head. "No, kid. Right now I got troubles of my own." He pushed the door open and walked from the stable, leaving the door open wide.

Billy hurried across the stable floor and pulled the door closed, locking it with an iron drop latch. He picked up a soft brush and went back to work grooming the horse, a wary, concerned smile playing on his lips.

Her smile seemed frozen. She looked, Tanner thought, uncannily like the portrait in John Tate's study. She was dressed in a gauzy, powder blue gown with long sleeves and a scooped neckline. A string of pearls graced her slender neck and a small gold charm bracelet her left wrist. Blue satin slippers were on her small feet.

"Eleanor, you were right," he insisted. "There are plenty of others who can look in on Carrie. You've got to believe me, though. I was not calling on her socially. She means nothing to me that way. You're the one I love."

"I believe you, Lee. I acted like a jealous shrew." She clasped his hand and led him to the sofa, where they sat side by side. "Forgive me, love." She placed her small hands on his cheeks and pulled his face close for a kiss.

"That goes double here," he agreed quickly. He had time for one more kiss before John Tate entered the parlor.

"Lee, it's been too long since we've had you out for dinner. Shame on you, Eleanor. I didn't raise you to be so neglectful."

"Daddy, Lee's been busy. He can't just drop what he's doing to come over and entertain me." She looked innocently up into Tanner's face and smiled. If she intended sarcasm, it was deliciously subtle.

"I hardly think Lee would consider it a chore." Tate seated himself on the edge of a chair. "Of course, I realize the day is fast approaching when you two will be having most every meal together."

If Tate was aware of Tanner's recent difficulties with his daughter, he was giving no indication.

"How are you coming along over there, anyway, Lee?" Tate asked, settling back gingerly in the hard-backed chair.

"I have about fifteen mounts ready to go. And the Army's contracted for them. They'll go at a pretty decent price, too. They're not just green broke. They are well-rounded horses, and they won't give them soldier boys any trouble."

"You must've worked night and day to get so many ready in such a short time."

"Lee's very dedicated and a hard worker," interjected Eleanor, pulling her slippered feet up on the couch and tucking them under the folds of her gown. She snuggled close against Tanner's shoulder. "It would take something pretty important to pull Lee away from his work. You don't have to worry, Daddy. I won't go hungry as long as he's around."

She smiled a sweet smile.

"One little problem, John," Tanner said. "Red tape is going to make payment for the horses about sixty days late. I'm going to have to make my first payment on the ranch out of that money I've got stashed away in your bank."

Tate shrugged. "No matter. I told you the bank could be very accommodating for the right individual." He grinned. "The bank can just wait for the payment until the horse money comes in. Besides—and just a small legal point—we shouldn't touch that money of yours. In the contract, we listed that money as part security for the loan."

Tanner frowned. "I had forgotten that. This isn't a very good way to start on a contract, is it?"

"I told you, son, don't worry. This kind of thing happens all the time when you're dealing in crops and livestock. The bank will not go broke because your eight hundred dollars is a few weeks late."

"I refuse to sit here and listen to any more of this," Eleanor declared. "Is there any other topic that interests you?"

"I'm sorry, my dear," Tate apologized. "You're right. How's your news sources in town, Lee?" he asked. "Sheriff making any progress on finding Troy's killer?"

Tanner shook his head. "He found a few hoofprints he's not sure about. He's looking for a horse to match. That's about all he's got that he's letting me in on."

"Is that so?" Tate's shaggy brows arched.

Tanner had a sudden image of Billy Tate rubbing down the fleet-footed animal in the stable. His instinct seemed to nudge him, and he searched quickly for a way to change the topic.

Eleanor obliged by saying, "This is wonderful, we move from banking to murder. Why can't we talk about something I might be involved in—like our wedding?"

"Are you sure you want to take a chance on scaring Lee off?" asked Tate, smiling. "Half the county has been invited. And, Lee, you don't strike me as a man who likes large crowds."

"Half the people on the guest list are your friends, Daddy—not mine," Eleanor put in cheerily. "Anyone would think you're celebrating a momentous event and wanted to show off. But I guess you're right. When a man finally marries off his spinster daughter, that is cause for celebration."

They all laughed at that, and the good humor continued through dinner. Even Billy, who joined them at the table, was unusually sociable.

When the evening was over and Tanner and Eleanor were finally alone, they clung to each other.

"Let's not do this anymore," he said. "Fight, I mean. It tears me up."

She laid her head on his chest. "I haven't slept hardly a

wink since Saturday. Oh, Lee, I love you so. I wouldn't let anything come between us."

He kissed her, wrapping his arms around her in an almost frantic grasp.

CHAPTER 17

TANNER sat down on the ground with his back resting against a boulder still warm from the sun, and felt his restlessness and tensions drain away. The hunting trip had been a good idea. He had needed this break, and he was glad Reynolds had come along. The sheriff was fairly good company away from the responsibilities of his office.

Three weeks had passed since the evening at the Tate's when he and Eleanor had reconciled. But he had ridden away from the clasp of her soft arms with a bitter taste clinging to his senses. He felt, as he had made his lonely way home, that he had compromised something very important to himself. Maybe even his manhood. Well, he thought, that was putting it too strongly. Maybe he had only bent himself a bit. But the feeling was there, and he couldn't shake it. They had joked, to be sure, about nagging wifedom, but the fear rode with him that maybe the bull ring for his nose she had kidded him about was more than figurative.

He had always felt he was his own man. He had formed his code early in life. And it was tested and tempered during his years in the war, when he was forced each day to fight and kill and make moral decisions with which he could live. He had told Eleanor his role in the Army had been that of a horse trainer. And that was true. What he did not mention was that he had spent two gruesome years in the thickest and goriest part of the fighting. And, somehow, amid all the blood and agony, he had come to know himself. He figured out who Lee Tanner was, and he liked the man.

Tanner's approach to life was simple. Accept each day on its own terms and live it to its fullest, never wish it away out of boredom, or because that day happened to bring pain. Accept people and horses as they are. You can't change people. You can train a horse, but when you're through, it's still a horse.

Tanner had made a lot of mistakes in his life. Each man makes his own mistakes, and each man must pay the price for those mistakes. But never should a mistake be allowed to drag you all the way down. Straighten it out if you can. And if you can't, forget it and go on. And do it all without whimpering or whining. This, in his simple reckoning, was the essence of being a man.

Now, Tanner felt he had compromised his principles in some way.

It was not just the issue of Carrie Farley, and the obligation he had felt to look after her. As he had said to Eleanor, there were others who could do that. It was almost as though . . . Tanner didn't know. Eleanor had the right to her own feelings, and that included jealousy and love and everything in between.

Reynolds's heavy step behind him jerked Tanner back. The sheriff came wheezing his way down the rocky path to the lonely boulder where Tanner sat. In each meaty hand he carried a steaming tin cup of coffee. He passed one of the cups to Tanner, found a friendly-looking piece of soil, and sat down.

"Purty, ain't it?" he mused, looking far away across the valley, now into the deep blush of the dying sun. High above, an eagle scolded its mate home to nest for the night. The shrill bugle of an elk echoed from higher up in the mountains behind them.

A chill night breeze was working up, and Tanner shivered, clutching the tin cup close, savoring the smell and warmth of the fresh coffee in the steam rising into his face. The green of the valley floor had turned to a purple velvet carpet.

"If a man can't appreciate this, there's somethin' serious wrong with him." Reynolds spat out his tobacco cud and watched it slide away down the hill a few feet. He sipped the scalding coffee.

The entire trip, however short, had been a good, restful time for both men. Tanner had awoken one morning to find himself exhausted. He needed rest. He owed himself a rest. The fifteen horses, the first produced on the Tanner ranch, were now safely in the hands of the Army. In the bank in Sweetwater was deposited an Army voucher in the sum of fifteen hundred dollars, redeemable in sixty days. The whole enterprise had gone off without a hitch, and Tanner decided it was time to reward himself with a few days away from the ranch.

"You know what I'm going to do, Tanner? I'm going to build me a cabin up here somewheres. And I'm going to use it winter and summer to get away from that town and its infernal people with their infernal problems."

Tanner said nothing. No response was needed for that kind of talk. Dream talk. Wish talk. No cabin would ever be built here by Reynolds. And it would quite likely be another ten years before he would again leave his town in the hands of a deputy and ride off into the mountains.

From off to their left, to the south, toward the 'Dobes, a coyote barked. A moment later, an answering cry drifted up from somewhere on the flatlands.

"Did you know I had me a family once, Tanner?" Reynolds set his cup on the ground, folded his hands across his ample belly.

"I was just countin' up," Reynolds continued. "It'll be fifteen years in June, next month, when Sarah took the boys and hightailed it."

"Well, now," said Tanner. "Ain't that a kick in the head?" He found himself intensely curious. Several questions came to his mind, but he waited.

Reynolds picked up his cup and threw the remainder of his coffee on the ground.

"I was a hell of a lot younger then, Tanner. And, goddamn,

was I stupid. My ever-lovin' pride. Lots of pride and no brains."

It was close to full dark now. Tanner's stomach growled, and Reynolds, as though catching the faint rumble, stirred.

"Aw, hell," the sheriff said, struggling to his feet. "Probably worked out for the best anyways. Women who don't understand lawmen got no business marryin' 'em."

They walked back to the fire, tended to the horses, hobbling them so they could graze among the scrub pine, and settled down to their dinner of roasted venison steak. The meat was excellent, for the buck was young and the steaks tender and juice-saturated. The smoke from the cooking fire had lent an extra spark to the flavor, a snap that no conventional seasoning could match. Each man polished off his steak with concentrated zeal.

After washing their tin plates and utensils, Reynolds produced a bottle of whiskey from his pack and both men settled back against their saddles. The whiskey loosened their tongues, and they talked long and hard, deep into the night.

After they had finished the bottle, brought in the horses, and then banked the fire and rolled into their blankets, Tanner lay thinking about his rapidly approaching wedding. It was less than two weeks away now. Eleanor seemed to be growing more frantic by the day. Her temper seemed in constant evidence, as she snapped at Tanner, her father, Charlotte, almost everyone who came within range. And just as abruptly as the outbursts, her apologies would follow, generally accompanied by a flood of tears.

Once the wedding was over, she would be fine, Tanner assured himself.

Tanner's eyes had closed, his body relaxed, ready for sleep, when a thought jerked him back. He recalled the strange light he had seen burning in Eleanor's eyes of late, and it shown particularly bright on the evening when he mentioned to her about camping in the mountains a couple of days with Reynolds. Her brow had forrowed. She seemed suspicious, as if she didn't believe Tanner. Did she suspect he was seeing Carrie? he wondered. After a moment she had seemed to shake the mood, and she came lovingly into his arms.

"I shall miss you," she murmured. "Be careful."

In the morning he and Reynolds must go back, no matter what. The youngster from town Tanner had hired to look after the stock would be expecting him. Reynolds, as willingly as he had soaked up the relaxation, would be anxious to get back and check on his town.

Tanner dozed, settling deeper into the blankets as the chill night breeze toyed with the embers around the edges of the fire.

Neither man spoke as they rode, ambling along into the lower country, stopping now and then to allow the horses to grab a mouthfull of grass. They reached the valley floor, and the grass that had appeared so green from above took on a green-gray hue, like seawater.

It was Reynolds who first spotted the rider. He watched silently as the lone horseman, a flyspeck on the horizon, cut the distance between them. He said nothing until Tanner, too, had noticed and then they drew rein together.

"Whoever the hell that is, he's burnin' that horse up at both ends," said Reynolds, loading his cheek with a fresh wad of chew. They waited and watched as the rider drew nearer.

"That look like the rider you give chase to, Tanner?"

Tanner knew immediately that it was not. "Once you've seen that horse run, you'd never forget it."

They rode ahead slowly. Abruptly, Reynolds spoke up. "Hell's fire. That's Davis."

Both men touched spurs to their mounts and rode swiftly ahead through the swaying grass to meet the sheriff's deputy.

Shots carried to them. The deputy was firing his pistol in

the air. He was close enough now that they could see him spurring his lagging horse.

When the deputy pulled to a ground-churning halt, his horse, a large-boned buckskin, staggered and nearly fell. Then the horse locked its legs, fighting for its wind with laboring lungs.

"You tryin' to windbreak that horse? You better have a goddamn good reason for runnin' an animal like that." The sheriff spat a stream off into the tall grass.

"Good enough, Sheriff, I reckon." Davis himself was haggard, grim-faced, and drenched with his own sweat. "You said you'd be comin' in sometime this mornin', but I figured you'd want to know as soon as possible."

"Damn it. Are you goin' to tell me?" asked the sheriff irritably. "Or do you want me to guess?"

Davis swallowed hard, fighting, like the horse, for his breath. "Farley place burnt last night, Sheriff. Burnt to the ground. Andy Farley's dead. Carrie's burnt real bad. She's at Doc's, and he don't know if she'll live."

CHAPTER 18

REYNOLDS discharged his wad of chew over the side of the horse. "What in the hell are you talkin' about?"

"How bad is Carrie?" Tanner asked, his heart clamoring against his ribs.

A bit of color was returning to the deputy's cheeks. "She ain't burnt so bad, but she inhaled a bunch of smoke. Doc fears she maybe singed her lungs."

"How in damnation did it get started?" Reynolds asked.

Davis shook his head. "That we got to figure out, Sheriff. One of the hands—that kid, Rawlins—he woke up and it looked to him like the whole place had gone off at once. He ran out in only his skivvies and pulled Carrie out. Tried to get to the old man, but the whole place was fallin' in by then. The kid's all gouged and cut up."

Tanner was the first to react. He pulled his sheath knife, reached behind, and cut loose the ropes holding the deer across the Appaloosa's rump. The carcass dropped into the grass with a *whump*.

"I don't know about you," he said to the sheriff, "but I'm going in to see how Carrie's getting on. Maybe I'll see you later at the ranch." The big Appaloosa was moving out before he had a chance to touch a spur.

Reynolds watched Tanner ride away.

"You come on back to the Farley ranch," Reynolds told the deputy. "But take your time, for God's sake. Go easy on that horse, or you'll be walkin' in."

He put his own horse into a gallop, headed due west for the Farley ranch.

When Tanner arrived, Carrie Farley lay on the bed, eyes closed, covered only with a light sheet. Her arms were swathed in gauze bandages. The right side of her face was encased in a glistening coat of grease, beneath which were angry blisters and reddened flesh.

"These burns are superficial," said Doc Brennan. "It's what's happened to her throat and lungs that worries me. Even if a person survives something like this, they're usually plagued with all kinds of miseries farther down the road."

"What do you mean?" Tanner shook his head numbly.

Doc Brennan threw foul-smelling swabs into a trash bucket, and washed his hands in a basin as he explained.

"The lungs probably have been burned by the hot air and smoke she inhaled. The first problem we might encounter—and remember, I said might—is fluid building up in the injured lungs, causing pneumonia and, in effect, drowning her. Another problem might be heavy scarring, bringing on a variety of other lung ailments—consumption, for example."

Tanner passed a weary hand over his eyes. He felt as if he was losing touch with reality.

"Sit down over here," the doctor said gently. He pointed Tanner to a chair beside a small desk. "No matter what happens," he concluded, "it will take several days before we really know which way it's going to go."

"It's down to that?" Tanner asked, looking up into a face mapped with campaign lines from a thousand battles. "She might die?"

"It's a possibility." Brennan smiled a little. "When I first saw her, I'll admit I was ready to call for Peavey. But I got her cleaned up, saw that glint in her eyes. . . . I'm counting on her making it."

Tanner looked again at the small, pitiful form. "Starting to be one hell of a bad year for that little gal," he said.

"No one is going to argue with you there," Brennan agreed.

Tanner picked up his hat and moved slowly to the door.

"Doc, there's still enough daylight left. I'm going out and meet the sheriff at the Farley ranch. See if he's figured out yet how the fire got started." He looked at the doctor's haggard face. "As soon as I do that and make arrangements to have the kid stay over that's taking care of my stock, I'll come back and sit with her overnight."

The Appaloosa looked ragged. Dried sweat crackled on its flanks and chest, caked mud on its fetlocks. The spring had gone out of its stride. It longed to be home, eating its sweet hay and resting. But it would go where the man directed. It would go until it arrived or until it dropped dead. In part, its emotions were imparted to it from the man. So long had they been together, at times it seemed the two, man and horse, had become one feeling unit. Now the Appaloosa felt unsteady, apprehensive. The man was worried.

Tanner arrived at the Farley ranch before dusk. As he rode in, he passed Tim Rawlins, forking hay over the fence to a dozen soon-to-calf heifers.

Rawlins's hands were bandaged, and he held the pitchfork handle gingerly. He looked up at Tanner and waved one bandaged hand. "Mr. Tanner. How ya doin', sir?"

"Well, son, I look to be doing a sight better than you." He smiled at the youngster. "That was a brave thing you did for Carrie. If she pulls through, it'll be because of you."

The young man's cheeks reddened. "Man does what he's got to do," he muttered, looking off into the distance. It was apparent he was pleased at the compliment.

Tanner waved and rode on, stopping and dismounting at the edge of the burn.

Deputy Davis had built a small fire of the scattered pieces of singed wood and was hunkered down, warming his hands over the flames. The sheriff stood, one foot on a charred beam, a grim expression frozen on his face.

Reynolds stagger-footed over to join Tanner, stepping over

live embers and debris. His face was grimed with sweat and ash.

He shook his head at Tanner. "From the looks of it, she damn near all went at once. Andy never even had a chance to get out of bed."

"You think it was set deliberate?" Tanner asked.

"Hard to say." Reynolds squinted and wiped at his sweaty face and eyes with his bandanna.

"Hey, Sheriff," called Davis. He was squatted on his haunches near his little campfire, a small piece of charred wood pressed to his nose. "What do ya make of this?"

He tossed the chunk of wood to Reynolds. The sheriff caught it deftly in his left hand. A faint, oily aroma touched his nostrils.

"Kerosene," he muttered, and handed the chunk to Tanner. "Well, that answer your question?"

Tanner sniffed at the wood and passed it back.

"Two questions left now. Who and why?"

At two o'clock in the morning, Carrie moaned softly and opened her eyes. A little cry escaped her cracked lips.

Tanner had been dozing in the hard, unforgiving desk chair, but was awake and went to her side instantly.

Her eyes focused slowly, searched his face for a moment, and then gleamed in recognition. She tried to smile but managed only a lopsided grimace. A wave of pain passed over her face, like a ripple over a pond, and she moaned again.

"Tanner, it hurts," she whimpered.

He reached for a small brown bottle on the bedstand. "Doc said if you woke up I was to give you this."

He uncorked the bottle, placed a gentle hand beneath her head, and coaxed her to swallow a little. When he laid her down again, he saw that her eyes were closed. She had passed out.

Tanner stood for a while by the bed, listening to Carrie's

even breathing. Brennan had said to listen for a rattle in her lungs. That could mean immediate problems, perhaps strangulation. In that event, Tanner was to turn her on her side and come upstairs to wake him immediately.

Carrie's breathing was shallow, but it sounded clear and unimpeded to Tanner.

He returned to his chair and, with an elbow resting on one chair arm and head cradled in his hand, he tried again to doze.

This time sleep escaped him. With the discovery of the kerosene-soaked wood, it was now virtually certain that the fire had been set. And it was an equal certainty, in Tanner's mind at least, that the one who had started the fire was the same person responsible for the death of Troy Sams. Of course, there could be more than one individual involved, but Tanner had a feeling both murderous acts were tied to the rider on the dark horse.

Tanner was almost sure that the rider was Billy. Therein lay one hell of a dilemma. To report his suspicions to Sheriff Reynolds and tell him about seeing Billy on the thoroughbred mare was certain to open up a hornet's nest all the way around. The sheriff would show up on Tate's doorstep, questioning his son on information volunteered by Tanner; this would most surely upset John Tate, not to mention Billy himself. It was easy to predict how Billy would react. Bad enough to have Tanner tattle to his father about his sneaking the mare out and running her, but to pass along information to the sheriff leading to Billy's being accused of having something to do with the murders of Sams and Andy Farley . . . Tanner could see Billy reaching for his gun and blowing all their lives to hell.

There was no real proof that Billy was involved, he grudgingly admitted. It could not be proven that it was he that had been at the site where Troy was killed. A few prints from a horse with small hooves might be enough to warrant questioning, but that was about all.

And finally there was Eleanor. As shaky as their relationship was at this point, Tanner knew he had better think long and hard before waltzing in and accusing her brother of anything.

At dawn, Tanner stirred himself from the chair and stretched. His buttocks had lost all feeling, and he felt certain several vertebrae had slipped sideways.

He rubbed his back and checked on Carrie for the hundredth time. The laudanum in the bottle had worked well, allowing her uninterrupted sleep for the most part. Her breathing had deepened and become more regular. Tanner took that as a good sign.

He walked stiffly to the little coal heater in the corner, worked the grate from side to side to sift down the ashes and freshen the cinders. He then placed a fresh pot of coffee on to brew.

At eight o'clock, Brennan arrived in the outer office, followed by a pretty, dark-haired girl in her late teens.

"This is my neice, Melody. She is going to play nurse to Carrie. Give both us old men a rest."

Tanner smiled approvingly. "Carrie's bound to improve faster with a good, capable woman looking after her. Men never did have a light enough hand for this kind of thing. No offense, Doc."

The girl blushed, pleased, and smiled shyly while taking off her coat in a get-down-to-business manner. She tied a small, white apron around her middle and stood by Brennan's elbow while he began his examination of Carrie.

The doctor's appearance had improved dramatically since last evening. He had shaved and he seemed fresh, and his movements were deft and sure.

When he finished, he nodded. "We're making headway. I particularly like the way the lungs sound."

He turned to Tanner. "Thanks for staying, Tanner. She's got a good friend in you. Now you go home and get some rest. There's no more you can do here. I'm going to have

Melody help me change the dressings and see if we can get some nourishment in her. Who's taking care of those horses of yours while you're in here lazying around?"

"Jeff Lewis. He's the youngster who helps out over at the livery. He stayed out at the place while Reynolds and I went on our camping trip." In his weariness, Tanner's voice sounded to him as though it were coming up from the bottom of a deep well.

He slipped into his coat, picked up his hat, and directed his dragging steps to the door. "I'll be talkin' to you later, Doc."

He stopped at the hotel long enough to eat a quick breakfast. As he was leaving, he brushed into Reynolds coming into the dining room.

"You move into town, Tanner?" the sheriff asked.

Tanner wearily explained that he had just come from Doc Brennan's.

"Our little camping trip was great, but it sure as hell ended on a sour note, now didn't it," Reynolds lamented. "Say, how's the girl comin' along?"

"Doc thinks she's making some real progress. Be a while before he can say for sure."

Tanner felt a pang of guilt. He wondered again if he was doing the right thing, keeping quiet about Billy Tate. He wondered, too, if his motives were on course. Was it an unwillingness to cast groundless suspicion on a man, or simply a wish to keep from soiling his own nest?

Second-guessing himself—he was doing a lot of that lately. Questioning. Doubling back.

"I got to go home and get some sleep," Tanner said, feeling a tightness in his stomach. "I'll ride in tonight and look you up for a drink."

When he reached home, the boy from the livery was sitting on the back steps of the house, concentrating on repairing an old leather headstall. He looked up as Tanner rode in, and he waved cheerily.

LEE TANNER ■ 133

"I got 'em all fed and seen to, Mr. Tanner. You sure got some nice horses here."

Tanner smiled at the boy and climbed from the saddle.

"These are not quite as nice as the ones I just sold to the Army," he said. "Didn't have any problems, I guess?"

"None 'tall. Soon's I get my bridle back together, I'll be on my way. Old Man Tucker will be wonderin' where in Hades I'm at. You goin' to want me to come back tonight?" he asked hopefully, swiping at the blond hair hanging limp and straight over his eyes.

"If you can make it, Jeff." He watched the boy wrestling with the old leather of the bridle. "You just sit tight a minute," Tanner said, and walked to the barn. He returned with a new bridle and new reins and tossed them across the boy's lap. "Switch your bit over to this," he said. "That old one ain't safe."

The boy looked up, startled, round eyes peering out through the tangle of hair. "Hell's fire, Mr. Tanner. I cain't . . ."

"Yeah, you can. Now switch that bit over and get your butt out of here so I can get some sleep. I probably won't be here when you get back tonight, so just follow through the way you been doing."

He laid a hand on the boy's shoulder as he passed up the steps and into the house.

"And put ol' Jake away for me, will you?" he called back over his shoulder before closing the door.

Tanner had nearly reached town that afternoon when the thought flashed upon him quick as lightning—he had promised Eleanor he would ride out to see her the very evening he returned from the camping trip. In all the confusion, that very important appointment had slipped his mind. Here he was, on his second trip to town, and she didn't even know he was back.

He cursed himself. As touchy as things were with that gal,

he certainly could not afford to antagonize her further. And the very reason he had not seen her was he was tending to Carrie, the one person he had promised Eleanor he'd steer clear of. He shook his head. How did things get so damn complicated?

He would see the sheriff, check on Carrie, and then ride out and spend the rest of the evening with Eleanor. The longer he waited, the greater the risk of stirring up her wrath. If Eleanor were to learn the reason he had not called, and she was almost sure to, she would want to know just why he had taken it upon himself to be so concerned with this girl. "And didn't she have the right to ask that?" Tanner asked himself out loud. "You love Eleanor. You're engaged to marry the lady." Yet, when he had heard the bitter news of the fire and Carrie's condition, it was like someone had delivered a blow to his stomach. He had nearly run Jake's legs off getting to town.

How could he not feel sympathy for Carrie? She had lost everything but the land and cattle. She could rebuild her home, but it would be empty with her father and Troy dead. It might make more sense for her to sell out and move to town.

He kicked the surprised Appaloosa into a lope. Someday, he hoped, he would learn to take care of his own affairs and stay the hell out of the problems of others. All of this began when he had helped a dying old man.

When he reached the sheriff's office, Reynolds had himself just arrived. He was washing his hands and face at a tin basin against the wall when Tanner walked in.

"Had supper yet?" asked the sheriff, combing the wet tangles from his large mustache and then giving his semibald scalp a perfunctory stroke with the comb.

Tanner shook his head. "I'll come along and have a cup of coffee with you and watch you eat."

"Off your feed?" asked Reynolds, slipping into his leather vest and putting on his hat.

"Feel like I got a pound of lead in my gut. I think it must be a holdover from your cookin' up on the mountain."

"It ain't that," Reynolds asserted. "It's what's called prenuptial butterflies. You got about . . . what, two weeks before the funeral? Uh-oh. Did I say funeral?" He grinned.

He closed the office door behind them, and they moved down the nearly deserted street. It was midweek, and traffic in town was light.

"Went back out to the Farley place today," said Reynolds after they were seated. "Never guess what I found out beyond them implement sheds."

"More tracks?"

Reynolds looked quickly at Tanner. "That's right."

The waitress brought the two men coffee, and the sheriff stirred sugar into his and glanced questioningly at Tanner.

"You know somethin' you ain't lettin' me in on," he said abruptly.

Tanner nodded. "I should've told you this earlier. But I wasn't sure just what it meant, and when you hear it you'll know why I held off."

"I'm listenin'."

"Keep it in mind it may not even be the same horse. But I don't . . . "

"Get on with it, Tanner," the sheriff ordered, exasperated.

"I saw Billy Tate on a horse that would match up pretty close with the prints you're talking about. As far as size goes, anyhow."

Reynolds had started to raise his cup. He set it back on the table and stared at Tanner.

"It's a thoroughbred filly. John Tate bought it a while back for racing and breeding."

"You think it's the right horse?"

Tanner considered a moment. "In my own mind, I do.

There can't be another like her around these parts. I know for damn sure it's the one I gave chase to."

Reynolds frowned. "Why do you suppose he's keepin' the horse under wraps?"

"I can't say," answered Tanner quietly. "Unless John Tate is aware of the problem. I mean—"

"I know what ya mean." Reynolds mulled it over for a moment, then shook his head. "If you're implyin' Tate thinks his boy is goin' around plinkin' people in the head and is tryin' to help cover it up—hell, I ain't buyin' it. John Tate wouldn't have no part in somethin' like this." He paused. "I can see why you might want to think twice before bringin' it up, though. John Tate's been good to you. You're gettin' set to marry his daughter. Hell of a way to repay a man."

Tanner flinched as though stung.

"Oh, hell, Tanner," Reynolds said, flustered. "That didn't come out right at all." A slow flush worked its way up the ample jowls. "You're caught in a hell of a spot, and you done the right thing."

"Time will have to answer that one," Tanner said gloomily. "What do you aim to do now?"

Reynolds's dinner of beef stew and biscuits was set before him. He tasted the stew and gave the waitress the okay sign.

"Guess I'll have to go out and take a look at that horse," he said, lathering a biscuit with butter and honey. "I'll try an' keep your name out of it if possible."

"You ask to see that horse and Billy's going to know exactly who you been talking to," Tanner said resignedly. "But you got to do it, I know."

Tanner finished his coffee and pushed away from the table. "When you going out?" he asked.

"Tomorrow," Reynolds answered, his mouth full.

"I'm going to ride out tonight to see Eleanor. I'll try to step around all this, but I would like to prepare her a little."

Reynolds nodded. "All right by me. Whatever's going on,

it won't concern her. Directly, anyways. And who knows, maybe it'll all check out."

Before leaving town, Tanner went to check on Carrie's condition. As when he had left her that morning, she was asleep.

"Best thing for her," Brennan assured him. "The laudanum has been working extremely well for the pain. She's comfortable enough. And I think we can put away our fears about her lungs. They appear quite sound. At least for now."

"You think she's going to be all right?" Tanner asked hopefully.

Brennan shrugged. "The only thing that has me concerned at the moment is there has been some damage to her vocal cords. I'm not sure what occurred—I don't see how they could've been burned. More than likely she's suffering an infection. Scar tissue seems to be forming." He thought for a moment. "Did she say anything last night? How did she sound?"

Tanner considered a moment. "She just kind of whispered."

Brennan nodded. "That might be as good as her voice is going to get," he said soberly.

"She might lose her voice? That's a hell of a deal, Doc."

"Yes, but last night," the doctor answered a bit defensively, "we weren't even sure she was going to live. As a trade, the deal is not bad—her voice for her life."

Tanner nodded. "You're right. Seems tough, though."

"Reynolds was by after you left this morning," said Brennan. "He said the fire was set deliberate. Now who in hell would want to do such a thing?"

Tanner looked thoughtful for a moment, shook his head, and moved to the door.

"I don't know," he answered. "But I got a feeling the son of a bitch is about out of rope."

CHAPTER 19

BILLY Tate was agitated. He sat on a bench in the horse barn with his back against an empty stall door, staring across the alley at the thoroughbred filly. He desperately wanted to ride the horse, but his father was home.

It was a bright sunny morning, five weeks after Troy Sams's murder. Billy was feeling the tension, as were many others. Most of the thirty or so hands of the Tate outfit, foreman Quince included, had withdrawn into themselves. The death of Kyle Bridges had not raised much of a stir, but Troy Sams, that was a different matter. Troy had been liked and respected. What's more, word had filtered out from the sheriff's office that whoever had committed the murder was more than likely an acquaintance or neighbor of the victim, and so a neighbor to them all. Of a sudden, everyone became suspect. Paranoia set its steely jaws in the back of each man's neck. Tempers grew short. The joking and horseplay ceased, and Billy Tate more and more found himself sitting alone.

Not that Billy had ever been well liked. He was certain that it was because of his status as the boss's son. The men tolerated him, even deferred to him, but he was never friends with any of the men. Quince alone had never paid homage to him. Quince treated Billy as if he were just another hand, to be ordered about at will. Oddly enough, this suited Billy just fine. He found in the big, strong-mannered man someone to admire—a man's man, not bent or easily intimidated. And someday, when Billy was running the show—the old man couldn't live forever—he would need a man like Quince.

The only thing standing between him and control of the ranch someday was Lee Tanner. It had long been anticipated,

by Billy at least, that he and Eleanor would share ownership
and that he would enjoy complete control over the ranch and
the rest of his father's enterprises. Everything was looking
up after Eleanor's argument with Tanner a month ago, but
they had made up the next week. Now, with Tanner in the
picture and the wedding a couple of weeks away, Billy felt his
future was slipping out of his fingers.

Tanner was fooling no one. The Whiteman place was just
the beginning. Lee Tanner, Billy suspected, was making
plans one day to live in John Tate's house and take over John
Tate's empire. And Billy Tate could take the hind tit and be
damned.

This whole fearsome idea gnawed at Billy with annoying
frequency. Since Tanner first showed up that night with
Rooster's body, Billy had felt Tanner was going to mean
nothing but trouble.

Eleanor was too nervous to sit still for long. She knew
Tanner was due home from his hunting trip and he would
be calling on her as soon as he returned. She wandered about
the study, basking in the solitude and the dark security of
old leather furniture, leather-bound tomes, dark-grained
woods, and the reek of ancient cigar smoke. The smell and
the feel were familiar to her from childhood.

She sat down at her father's massive desk and leaned back,
luxuriating in the rich leather comfort, studying the large
portrait of her mother on the opposite wall.

What an odd pair they must have been. Eleanor could not
recall a great deal about her mother. She had been four
when Justine Tate had died, only a year after giving birth to
Billy. In Eleanor's childhood images of her mother, she
could recall no loving touch, no nurturing, no comforting—
only strident, angry voices behind closed doors.

In contrast to her mother's coldness, her father had lav-
ished upon Eleanor love and indulgence. Charlotte had
taken care of mothering Eleanor and Billy, even before their

mother's death. But from Justine Tate, until the day she
vanished forever from Eleanor's life, there had not been so
much as eye contact with the little girl.

Eleanor reflected upon the portrait of the blond, beautiful
woman. Her mother. Her mother, the stranger.

We look much alike, Mama, she mused sadly. Maybe that's
why Daddy loves *me* so much. But you and I are not alike. I
love Lee and he loves me. We are going to be happy.

The portrait seemed to take on hard, cruel lines around
the eyes. The full lips seemed to press thin—the eyes to bore
into Eleanor's own.

Eleanor's face went white. Her eyes widened. She tilted her
head to one side.

"I know I've said that before, Mama," she murmured
through stiffened lips. "But Lee won't do that to me. He's
not like the others."

She sat bolt upright.

"I believe him! You'll see!" Angry tears welled in her eyes.
"Lee loves me! Only me!"

That evening, Tanner was surprised by how calmly Eleanor
took the news about his conversation with Sheriff Reynolds.
Maybe it was because she had already burnt her embers on
an earlier topic of conversation.

"You must have enjoyed your hunting trip to stay longer
than you had expected," she had said as they sat, holding
hands in the parlor.

Tanner's hackles were raised by the comment, but he was
determined to keep peace between them tonight, at least
until he had to shatter it with his suspicions about Billy.

"On our way back," he said, "the sheriff's deputy met us.
There was a terrible fire at the Farley place. Old Man Farley
was killed."

"Oh?" Eleanor's face flushed. "What about Carrie?"

Tanner was moved by her concern for the girl she had
once been so jealous of. "Carrie was seriously injured. In

fact, last night Doc Brennan wasn't sure she'd make it through the night, but now he thinks she'll survive."

"What!" she shrieked and jumped up from the settee, her back to Tanner.

"Eleanor, I'm sorry," he said, hoping to staunch the flow of her jealous rage.

"*You*'re sorry? About what?" she asked, turning to him. "What have you done?"

"Well, I spelled Doc last night—he was bone-tired when I got there, so I sat up with Carrie while he got some sleep."

She glared at him, her eyes narrowing. But instead of exploding in anger, she pulled a tight smile and said, "Well, of course you did. That's the kind of person you are, considerate and compassionate." She flung herself down on the settee beside him and said, "If you hadn't been so compassionate toward Rooster, a man you didn't even know, you would never have come into my life!"

Tanner could see that she was making a big effort to be gracious and understanding, and he loved her more now than he could have imagined possible.

"Darling," he said, settling her head on his shoulder, "I am so proud of you. Are you sure we can't get this wedding stuff done sooner?"

"Oh, Lee, is two weeks really such a long time?"

"I guess not," he had to admit. In fact, he hoped two weeks would be long enough to settle the waters after Loyal questioned the Tates about the horse tomorrow.

"Eleanor," he began, "I have to tell you something, and it isn't going to be easy. . . . "

After he finished she remained quiet, pensive. Then she stood up and said, "I think you'd better be going."

"Darling . . . " He reached out to her, but she pulled away.

"It's all right, Lee." She smiled at him, a cold and brave smile. "Billy can take care of himself."

* * *

John Tate slammed an angry fist on the desk as soon as the sheriff left. Tate sent his foreman to find Billy. "Tell him to get his butt in here! Right now!"

Quince found Billy striding, roosterlike, up and down the stone walkway leading from the ranch-house back door to the stable yard. He was looking down at his boots as he walked. He looked up when Quince approached.

"Hey, Quince," he called gleefully. "How do you like my new boots? They just finished making them yesterday."

Quince ignored the boots and the question.

"Your pa wants to see you, kid." He jerked a thumb in the direction of the house, then strode hurriedly on to the bunkhouse.

Billy needed to ask no questions. Quince's voice and the look in the foreman's eyes told him his father didn't want to see him to congratulate him on his fine choice of boots.

He entered the house with a leaden step, wended his way through the kitchen, the hallways, and paused outside the door to his father's study. He felt as if someone had implanted a large icicle within his bowels. He turned the knob with a wet palm and went in.

When he emerged, scarcely five minutes later, his face was ashen and he appeared dazed. He directed his faltering, confused steps to Eleanor's bedroom door.

She responded to his knock with an impatient scowl on her face. In her hand was a book, finger inserted between the pages.

"What is it?" she asked.

"The old man wants to see you."

She noticed for the first time the stunned look in her brother's eyes. She tossed the book in the direction of the bed. It struck the edge and fluttered to the floor like a stricken bird.

"What is it about?" Her voice was level and strong, but inside she quaked.

"What else? That goddamn horse."

Their eyes held for a moment.

She said finally, "I'll go right down."

Billy turned away and headed for the stairs.

Eleanor stepped back into the room, pressed her back tightly against the closed door, and stood with her eyes closed, trying to calm her fluttering heart.

Gradually, her pulse rate slowed. She stepped to the mirror and inspected a pale and drawn face with haunted eyes. She pinched her cheeks viciously until the color returned, then applied a brush to her hair until the static crackled.

At the top of the gleaming oak staircase, she paused and pressed a small fist into the pit of her stomach. A slight shudder passed through her frame. She descended the stairs.

She paused only a moment outside the heavy, carved door to her father's study, and then opened it without knocking and swept in.

"Reynolds was out this morning," John Tate said. "You know what he wanted?"

Eleanor sat down carefully in a chair before her father's desk. She nodded solemnly. "Lee told me last night."

"Did Lee tell you that it was he who first mentioned the horse to Reynolds?"

Again she nodded, her eyes remaining on the carpet. She was biting at her lower lip.

When John Tate had ripped into his son a few minutes before, his face had been a deep purple, suffused with rage. Now he was calm, his expression kind.

"If only Billy had not been sneaking rides on that horse," he said.

"Yes. If only . . ." she whispered.

He looked silently at her. She appeared beaten, her spirit exhausted. He slipped out of his chair and roll-walked his dwarfed body around the desk to his daughter's chair. He took one of her hands in his own.

"You are not to worry," he ordered. "There is nothing going on here that can't be ironed out."

Eleanor looked into her father's eyes, now elevated only slightly higher than her own. A single tear slid down her pale cheek.

"Here, here." He pulled her head against his chest and held her. "Not this way. I'll not have my girl carrying on this way," he crooned, as though to a small child.

"Can't you remember," he asked softly, "how many times Daddy has ironed out problems for his girl?"

Her shoulders shook with silent sobs. "It's all coming apart, Daddy!" She snuffled into his shirt front. "It was so wonderful for a while. . . ."

"It will be wonderful again, Eleanor. I'll take care of Lee Tanner and his accusations."

The door opened a crack and Charlotte peered in, neck craning, eyes squinting through her round spectacles. She took in the scene and started to retract her head, when John Tate glanced up and saw her.

"Come in, Charlotte," he beckoned.

The old woman hurried into the room, closing the door behind. She ran to Eleanor like a distressed brood hen.

"Why don't you take Eleanor to her room, Charlotte," Tate said, his voice husky. "She'll be all right now. I'm sure of it."

Eleanor raised her blond head and smiled weakly.

"Yes," she said, her voice catching. "I'm all right. Daddy, I'm sorry I came apart. I'll be stronger now. I promise." A shuddery sob escaped her, but she managed another smile.

John Tate reached up and kissed his daughter on one cheek. "You got nothing to be sorry for, Eleanor. Remember what I said. We can fix it."

She nodded weakly and allowed Charlotte to lead her to the door.

Before leaving the room, she paused once more.

"You're right, Daddy. We can fix it. You can fix it. I believe that now with all my heart."

John Tate did not miss the light in his daughter's eyes.

CHAPTER 20

TANNER was astride the young stallion, working it in tight circles and figure eights. He was applying cues, leg pressure at strategic moments, introducing the horse to the beginning of body communication with the rider.

The stallion had become a pet to Carrie, and she had asked Tanner to care for the horse while she was laid up. Carrie had done an excellent job thus far on the animal's training. All that remained now was the smoothing out, the finishing, putting miles under the saddle.

Rawlins and Parsons were the only two hands remaining on the ranch. They could be counted upon to feed the stallion and nothing more. Though his heart was not in it, Tanner had agreed to take the horse for a time.

It had been five days since he had told the sheriff about Billy and the horse. He had not heard from Loyal or from Eleanor, so he did not know how Loyal's visit with Tate had turned out.

But the matter weighed heavily upon him. He couldn't concentrate. He found himself giving the horse confusing signals, and, far worse, he was losing his temper frequently when the stallion did not respond correctly.

He dismounted, thoroughly frustrated, and was stripping off the saddle when Quince and Billy Tate rode into the ranch yard. They paused at the house, spotted him in the round pen, and rode over.

"Gotta message for you, Tanner," Quince said. "We're givin' you orders to vacate the property."

Tanner was stunned. He looked from Quince to Billy's

grinning face, and back to Quince. He asked, "Who's giving me orders to get out?"

"John Tate," answered Quince. "You got forty-eight hours."

"What's all this about?" Tanner demanded. "I'm not going anywhere on the say-so of you two."

"What it's about," sneered Billy, "is you plumb forgot to make your payment. It's now delinquent, and my dad is foreclosin' on yer ass!"

"Just hold up a damn minute. I offered to pay out of my reserve funds. He wouldn't accept it. He said the bank would wait on its money until the Army paid me for the horses. It was John Tate who suggested we do it this way!"

Quince shrugged. "You're free to ride over and discuss it with him. He just told me to deliver the message."

"And the message is," Billy cut in, "you got two days to pack up and get out. And we'll be back in two days to make sure. If we have to throw you off after that, we can do that, too."

Tanner's gaze frosted. "You know, Billy, if all this turns out to be like you say, you can count on one thing. I'll be here two days from now, just so I can see if you're man enough to throw me off the place."

"You got yourself an appointment." Billy glared at Tanner, then jerked the horses's head around and raked its flanks with his spurs.

Before turning to follow Billy, Quince said, "This wasn't my idea, Tanner. Just followin' orders."

Tanner nodded. "What's the deal, Quince?"

The big man shook his head. "Other than what I told you, I got no idea. Your best bet is to go talk to Tate."

He wheeled his horse about and rode out after Billy Tate.

Tanner rode into town that afternoon and dismounted in front of the bank. For a moment he stood by his horse, arm resting across his saddle.

He was suddenly very weary. He had no heart for a confrontation now with Tate or with anyone else. He couldn't seem to concentrate. He was unarmed, totally, and he was preparing to do battle.

He directed his leaden steps through the door into the cool interior. There were three cages, and only one was occupied.

A tall, slender man with a hatchet face and a dark smudge of a beard looked up at Tanner's step. "Mr. Tanner. Good day to you, sir."

Tanner nodded. "I'd like to see Mr. Tate if he's in."

"He left word he's expecting you. Go right on back."

Tanner pushed through the gate of the wooden railing that separated the customer area from the business and work area. He paused a moment before a heavy, carved door. He took a deep breath, knocked, and entered.

John Tate was at his desk. When Tanner entered, Tate looked up and then returned to his papers without comment. The quick glance he had shot Tanner had been expressionless.

Tanner crossed the room, steps muffled by the thick carpet. He took a seat in the straight-back chair before the desk.

"Guess we got some talking to do, John."

Tate looked up. His eyes appeared tired, uninterested. "All I can do is to repeat what I directed Quince to tell you. You have forfeited on your contract. The bank's trust in you was marginal, at best. Had I not vouched for you, the deal would never have gone through at all."

"I realize all that," Tanner answered carefully. "We both did. And from the start you made it plain to me that I had your blessing. And you said my being late on the payment wasn't important. You know I'm good for it, John. Hell, the money from the Army should be here next week at the latest."

"It's a pity," said Tate evenly. "The bank can wait no longer."

"But goddamn it, you got my two thousand! That should cover the payment and any late charges!"

"The two thousand was put up as security. In reality, once a payment is in default, the entire sum of the loan can be called in. The two thousand cannot be taken back and used again. I explained this to you already. And I know you don't have the full amount needed to satisfy the loan. But I tell you what—" Tate opened a drawer and withdrew a large envelope. "Here is the money you put up. You're out nothing."

"What the hell are you talking about?" Tanner shouted. "What about all the work and time I've put in?"

"A man takes risks. Life is like that."

"How could you do this one week before the wedding?"

"There will be no wedding."

Suddenly, Tanner put the pieces together. He was being dismissed, by Eleanor as well as her father.

"You used me like a pawn, you bastard! And now you're throwing me out! What I want to know is why. What have I done?"

"No one is using you, Lee. And you have done nothing other than fail to live up to a contract." He handed Tanner the envelope. "Here. Take your money. I'm very busy."

"It's because of Eleanor. Why don't you admit it?" He was speaking in a whisper now, chest heaving in anger. "You and Eleanor wanted something from me—that's why the glad-hand treatment. Now something's gone haywire and you're dumping me."

"My daughter's personal relationships have nothing to do with this matter. Any problems you have with Eleanor are between the two of you."

"You're a goddamn liar," Tanner said. "You cater to Eleanor's every whim. She's given you orders to get rid of me, and you've done it."

Tate shook his head. "I've got no more time for you. I've got a meeting to attend."

"All right," Tanner said, his face strained with emotion. "Do me one last favor, will you, John?" He moved to the door, placed a hand on the knob. "Tell Eleanor for me that she can go straight to hell!"

CHAPTER 21

TANNER rode the Appaloosa until full dark. He rode in a daze, unthinking, without regard for the failing horse beneath him. He was unaware of everything but the throbbing pain he felt inside.

The Appaloosa stumbled, and a few moments later stumbled again. And finally it was Lee Tanner's lifelong concern for horses that made him resurface from his own backwash of misery.

He was again mindful of the faithful horse that carried him, mindful of the unforgiving fact that animals that served man must be cared for; the one he rode, those in the pens at the ranch. For now, at least for tonight, he was their only provider. He turned toward home.

After feeding the stock, he entered the back door, built a fire in the kitchen stove, and put on a pot of coffee. He didn't think he could eat anything tonight, but a good hot cup of coffee had helped many a man through a hard spell. This, he fervently hoped, was as hard as it was ever going to get for him.

He realized he needed to sit down and draw up some new plans. The long range could wait: his immediate future was in question.

As he waited for the coffee to boil, he began sorting things out. The horses in the corral, unbroken stock and brood mares mostly, belonged to the bank, or to Tate. Yet Tanner could not just ride off and leave them. He was quite sure the Army would take the green stock, although one of their own men would have to do the breaking. He thought he might suggest this course of action to Quince.

He had Carrie's stallion to return to her. He would take care of that tomorrow.

About himself, he was sure of only one thing—he did not want to stay in the valley. At this moment, he felt the only hope for his sanity lay in getting as far away as the Appaloosa could carry him. He had nearly two thousand dollars, and the weather for traveling was certainly more accommodating than when he had first fought his way across the Cut Throat.

When the coffee boiled, he poured himself a cup. With the coffee in one hand, lantern in the other, he wandered about the house, through, as he now saw them, the foolishly fancy rooms of his and Eleanor's dreams. Melancholy attacked him. At one point, he felt almost sick with despair.

He no longer tried to make sense of why this was happening. It was now the rending reality with which he must do battle. Like some savage, blood-lapping beast, misfortune was after him to bring him down, and he must fight the beast, as he had following the death of his wife and children. Fight it, or it would consume him.

The next morning, Reynolds handed Tanner a cup of coffee, in the chipped porcelain cup. Tanner had told him about being evicted by Tate.

"So you're pullin' up stakes, eh?" The sheriff squinted at Tanner through the smoke of the pipe he was laboring to get started. "I'm real sorry to hear that, Tanner." He dropped one more burned out match and struck another. "I don't ever want to say nothin' against Eleanor—John Tate neither, for that matter—but that's a mighty high-strung young lady. Been that way all her life. I was a bit juberous about you and her from the start."

Tanner shook his head in frustration. "Eleanor's all messed up, Loyal. She's got the wrong slant on things. There was never anything between Carrie and me. Now she seems to blame me for telling you about Billy."

"Don't take offense, Lee," said Reynolds softly, "but I've always wondered if maybe Eleanor didn't inherit a bit of her mama's craziness. She flies off the handle so goddamn easy. Her and that brother of hers both."

"Did you happen to come to any conclusions on that horse of Tate's?" Tanner asked. "I understand you went out and had a look."

"Nothin' conclusive. If I'd only had a definite print to match up with, rather than having to rely on my memory of the tracks. Besides, even if it was the same horse at the site of the killings and the Farley fire, it still don't prove Billy was the one ridin' it. Could've just as easy been one of the hands. If Billy could sneak the horse out, anybody could. And you said yourself, the times you saw the horse and rider together, they weren't necessarily threatenin'."

Tanner nodded. "Might not even be tied in at all. Just an uneasy feeling I had."

They were silent while Tanner contemplated the dregs in the bottom of his cup. Reynolds appeared to concentrate on building an uninterrupted plume of smoke.

"Any idea which way you might be headed?" Reynolds asked presently.

Tanner shrugged and set the cup on the desk and picked up his hat. "Man without a star at the moment." He moved to the door. "I'll come by and see you before I leave."

"You do that, Tanner."

The morning was nearly gone when Tanner finished buying supplies at the mercantile. He kept it meager, filling two small canvas bags with easy-to-prepare trail food and extra ammunition for rifle and pistol.

He tied the two bags together at the necks by a stout piece of rope and draped them across the rump of the Appaloosa behind the saddle. When he added his bedroll, he and the horse would be trail ready.

For a moment he stood at the hitch rack, pondering whether or not he was hungry enough to eat something. He realized he was, but first he wanted to look in on Carrie.

When Tanner entered her room, Carrie was sitting up in bed, propped up with pillows. Her hair had been brushed and some of the brown curls had been arranged to cover the singed areas on the right temple. The skin on her right cheek was covered with angry red blotches. But her eyes looked clear, almost radiant.

"Now, look at you," Tanner said, dropping his hat on a chair. "You look like you're about ready to fight again."

Her blistered, peeling lips spread into a wide smile. "I'd fight you any day of the week," she croaked. Tanner had to lean forward to understand the words. "Just don't ask me to sing yet."

Tanner laughed. Her first words proved valid Brennan's concern over her voice. She seemed to find it necessary to capture air, expel it in a concentrated force in order to make sound. Each time she spoke it was a planned effort. Her voice had lost much of its feminine flow and resembled now, in pitch and tonal quality, the voice of a boy reaching puberty.

"How does Doc say you're doing?" Tanner asked, perching on the edge of the bed.

She gathered in strength, and croaked, "He's still worried about the lungs." A long pause. "Lungs feel okay. But I'm in no hurry to get out of here."

"Folks are lined up waiting to take you in. You can stay anywhere you want until you get your house rebuilt."

She shook her head. "I don't know. Maybe sell out. Dad's sister in Denver . . . and her husband would take me in. . . ." Her voice quit, and she looked up at Tanner helplessly. She seemed embarrassed.

"This is your home, Carrie. You have friends here. It'll sadden a lot of folks if you go away."

She nodded, silent, looking at her hands resting on the covers. Tanner guessed she was tiring.

When she looked up, her eyes were tearful.

"I don't believe what I've been hearing about you," she said in a gravelly whisper. "You're giving up. You're letting Tate run you out?"

"Good God!" exclaimed Tanner. "Is there anyone in this town that doesn't know my business?"

"I suppose you were just going to creep out of town?" Her voice, under the extra emotional strain, was already beginning to deteriorate. Her frustration was evidenced by her balled fists and flushed features.

"I was going to come and say good-bye," answered Tanner defensively. "Anyway, I'm glad you decided to stay," he said. "You belong here."

"How would you know where I belong?" she whispered savagely. "Oh, I'll stay, all right. And I'll survive. But everything is pointless and stupid."

"You've got your home, and the ranch. You can—"

"My home is gone, Tanner!" she croaked in frustration. "Some maniac burned it—along with my father! Reynolds says it may be the same maniac who killed Troy. It's as though someone is deliberately trying to destroy me."

Tanner reached for her hand, gave it a reassuring squeeze.

"You're too strong, Carrie. No one can destroy you. You've got to keep fighting. Don't give up."

She jerked her hand free from his clasp.

"Look who's talking!" she mocked angrily. "You're so full of good advice, Tanner. Keep fighting. Don't give up. Brave talk from a man who has his bags packed and his horse saddled."

A red flush mounted his cheeks, and he was on the point of an angry reply when it struck him that she was exactly right. What right did he have to advise someone to hold fast when it might get her killed? He was cutting and running, so why the hell shouldn't she?

"It's a little different with me, Carrie," he said lamely. "I got nothing left. No place to go. I got nothing to fight for."

Carrie looked at him with near contempt, her eyes filled with angry, unspilled tears.

"I'm not worth staying for?" she asked weakly. "A good friend like me?"

Tanner bowed his head helplessly. How could he make her understand? If it had been different, if he had met her first, if she had not been committed to his friend. It was too much. He couldn't handle it now. He had been bucked off and kicked good. Inside he felt like one large bleeding wound, feeling pain he was sure would never fade or diminish. And, in God's name, how could he take all this and lay it on this girl's doorstep?

"We could help each other, Tanner," she said, as if in answer to his last anguished question. The tears actually began to spill. "We could build the ranch together. My ranch—our ranch."

"Oh, God, Carrie," he groaned. "If only it could have been that way from the beginning. I knew deep down inside that Eleanor was a fantasy—just wishful thinking. I just wouldn't admit it. I wanted so bad to believe in it. Don't you see, Carrie, I can't just jump over now, as if all the rest had never happened."

"I guess that does it, then." Her green eyes were angry cat's eyes, and her strained whisper cut like a knife. "You know, Tanner, you disgust me. Despite the fawning over Eleanor and the bowing to the Tates, I always thought you were your own man. Until now."

Tanner sat staring at her, angry and confused.

What right had she to talk to him like that? Who was she to judge him?

He got up, snatched up his hat, and left. Outside, he stood for a moment, considering whether he still felt like eating.

"To hell with it," he muttered, turning back to the Appaloosa, feeling more empty and nauseous than before. "And to hell with her!" If she wanted to feel that way, that was her business. He had no control over other's opinions. It's what he thought of himself that counted. And, he admitted, though reluctantly, what he thought of himself at the moment didn't amount to much.

CHAPTER 22

THE first and most busying task of any lawman investigating a crime is asking questions. The bulk of his responsibility is finding, either directly or indirectly, the answers to those questions.

Sheriff Reynolds liked to ask his questions directly, without subterfuge or guile. Most questions, he found, are routine; few are dangerous. The wisest and oldest lawmen make a science of telling which are which. And Reynolds had been around a long time.

Sheriff Reynolds asked a question. It should not have been a dangerous question, but for him it proved fatal. He had asked about a horse. And in asking about that horse, he had set the machinery in motion.

Ordinarily, Reynolds was not a man easily frustrated, a slow-moving, implacable bloodhound. Generally, he found most of the answers he looked for. He was faced now with a situation that was not a bit to his liking. He had to admit, in this one instance, he had found no answers at all. And if he must call it as it lay, he would have to own up, with some embarrassment, that the one small break in the case had come from Tanner, and not through his own efforts.

After Tanner left his office, Reynolds sat at his desk for a time, drinking coffee and thinking. It seemed unlikely that Billy Tate could ride out on that damn horse like some avenging angel, wreak havoc, ride home, and go back to being the obnoxious, snot-nosed brat he was, all without the knowledge of John Tate. Reynolds felt his own assessment of the older Tate had been accurate. The man simply would not cover up a specter like that, son or no. Innocent people were dying.

But who else? One of the other hands? He shook his head. That, too, was unlikely. Yet the more he pondered it, the more certain he was that it was Tate's horse whose tracks had been found at the murder sites. Who the rider was, and whether or not he was involved in the murders, was a matter to be proven either way. And the very bottom line to it all was motive. Why would Billy, or anyone at the Tate ranch, turn to murder? What profit? What gain at all? What provocation?

He pulled his feet from off the desk top and stood up. The only thing he could do was go back to the Tates'. To snoop. To listen. To observe. The only gleam of light at all in this thing had come from under that bushel. He reached that resolve with a leaden heart, for, with even his limited political horse sense, he knew it was just not wise to fool with the Tates.

It was early afternoon when Reynolds rode into the ranch yard. John Tate, he knew, would not be at the ranch. Most days, except for Sunday, he would be found in his office at the bank. It was just as well, for when he again broached this particular subject with the elder Tate, Reynolds wanted to have a little more at hand than blind suspicion.

At the Tates', there was no movement at all that Reynolds could see. A single horse stood, hip-shot, in a pen close by, awaiting reshoeing, Reynolds guessed. A glance at the open forge seemed to bear this out, for it was red with coals. A large forging hammer lay at rest across the anvil. Where the farrier was, Reynolds had no clue. Probably in having coffee, or taking care of nature's business. The rest of the hands would be out working.

He rode past the blacksmith shop to the stable before dismounting. Glancing around once more, he pulled one of the large double doors open a space and slipped into the cool, shadowy interior. Once his eyes adjusted, he could see quite well. A certain amount of light filtered down from the three large cupolas on the roof.

There were perhaps sixteen or twenty stalls in the two rows, with a wide alley between. All were empty save the one containing the thoroughbred filly. It was housed near the center, on Reynolds's left as he entered.

The filly whinnied softly and tossed its fine head at the sheriff's approach. It was a dream horse at that. He took in once more its sleek lines with an admiring eye. It was a horse any man would sacrifice much to own. That fact might help to explain John Tate's secrecy concerning the filly. Horse thieves were by no means extinct in the Sweetwater valley. And one did not steal what one did not know to exist.

He stopped in front of the stall gate, and the filly reached its velvet nose over, timid but inquiring.

"Just like a woman," Reynolds chuckled. "Flirtin' with anything in pants."

The horse's swiftly moving lips searched his upturned palm for an offering, found nothing, lost interest, and pulled back to view the man from within the safety of the stall.

"Just like a goldang woman," he repeated.

He undid the latch and stepped into the stall, to the wary concern of the filly. He noted by the animal's calm eyes that it was not frightened, only careful, and he approached it with caution, hand extended toward its neck, not toward its head.

It allowed him first to touch and then to stroke the smooth coat, tossing its head about, indifferent to his offer of friendship. The man had no treats, therefore the horse was uninterested in pursuing the acquaintance.

Reynolds stooped, slipped his hand down the delicate foreleg to above the hoof. He squeezed the tendon in back of the fetlock, and the filly obediently raised its leg and placed its small hoof in his hand. Unbelievably small, too small, he mused, to give adequate support for a good working horse. But this was no stock horse. It would never be loaded down with someone of Reynolds's bulk. Those legs, hooves, and tendons would never have to stand the stress and strain of cutting cows from the herd or the shock of a steer at the end of a rope. This horse was royalty, meant for the king's road and the sport of kings.

Reynolds paid particular attention to the shoes, noting with admiration the perfect shoeing job, perfect shaping, perfect placement. If he were ever to see those mysterious hoofprints again, he would know for sure whether or not they had been made by this horse.

He set the horse's front hoof on the ground and moved along its side to the rear of the stall. Again the filly responded, raising its right rear leg with almost bored tolerance.

He was stooped, examining the hoof, when he heard the slight movement behind him. He thought it was the filly, growing impatient with his probing. This was his last thought, as a heavy forging hammer crushed his skull.

John Tate staggered into his study, locked the door behind him, and leaned back against it, eyes closed. He was sweating heavily, his hands were dirt-caked, and his custom-tailored suit was soiled. The tops of his boots were covered with fine dust.

When his trembling had slowed, he pushed away from the door and lurched across the room to the cabinet where the liquor was kept. The crystal decanter clattered against the glass as he poured.

The whiskey made fire in his belly. A moment later followed a warming, reassuring glow, flowing outward into his arms and legs, numbing and calming his racing brain.

Moving more slowly this time, he crossed behind the desk, whiskey decanter in hand, and sat down in his elevated chair.

As he sat and drank, he replayed his role of the last fifteen minutes, from where he had first driven up to the house.

He had noticed the horse first, tied before the stable door, and then the open stable door. The horse he didn't recognize immediately. Nonetheless, he had been filled with a vague dread.

He had crawled from the buggy and tied the bay to the hitch rack by the house, and then walked down the rocky path to the stable area.

He had stuck his head into the open doorway and peered down the alley between the stalls. His eyes loomed large, like those of a night frog, as they swept this way and that. Only the filly moved, wild-eyed, tossing its head and mane angrily.

He eased his way down the alley to the thoroughbred's stall, calling soothingly.

Tate continued speaking softly to the horse. At last it seemed to quiet some, standing to the right of the stall, pawing the clay floor and blowing through its nostrils.

His first look within served only to confuse him, for it seemed someone had tossed into the stall a pile of old and dirty rags. And then out of those rags took shape arms, legs, boots, and a great deal of blood.

Tate stifled an impulse to scream, clutching the stall gate for support. His wild eyes searched about the barn, the open rafters and beams above, the empty stalls and alley, everywhere but in the stall where that terrible thing lay.

Somehow he fought down the panic. The idea worked its way through his blind fear that here was a situation that he must deal with. He forced himself to look at the battered body of Sheriff Loyal Reynolds. The one visible staring eye seemed to probe a far corner of the stall, while one outstretched hand clutched at nothing.

Tate cast an uneasy glance at the horse, perplexed. A dead body and a horse. But the thing did not balance. The horse was spirited—but a killer?

A lead rope with a metal snap at one end hung from a nail next to the stall. Tate retrieved it and entered the stall, heart fluttering dangerously, and moved carefully to the horse's head. He held his breath, reached out with the snap end of the rope, and clipped it to a ring in the leather halter. His task now was to lead the animal from the stall and secure it in another while he tried to piece out some plan of action.

As he turned, his foot struck a heavy object. He stooped and picked up the forging hammer and stared unbelieving at the matted hair on its striking base.

A groan escaped him, and his sallow flesh turned even whiter. In one horrible instant he realized what had happened. He tossed the hammer aside and hurriedly led the filly from the stall. When he had the horse secured in another stall, he returned to the body. He must do something, and quickly, and though his heart pounded, he directed his disciplined banker's mind to the problem.

He considered first leaving the body where it lay, hiding the hammer, and telling Deputy Davis the horse must have kicked Reynolds to death after the sheriff had unwisely ventured into the animal's stall.

The idea was rejected on one main point: if at all possible, things must be arranged so that the sheriff's death would not be tied in with the ranch.

His mind scanned several possibilities. All left one or two strings hanging.

When he was near frustration, an idea occurred to him that amazed him with its simplicity and yet held, with the promise of total effectiveness, the added bonus of near-perfect safety for himself and the ranch.

He set about immediately to put the plan into effect.

John Tate was not a strong man physically, but under the stress of the moment he managed to accomplish a feat that would otherwise have been impossible for him. Stooping and grasping Reynolds's boots, he began dragging the body with a series of jerks from the stall, down the alleyway toward the door and outside the barn. He continued maneuvering the body until it lay beside the sheriff's horse.

He dropped the sheriff's boots, and they hit the ground

with a *thump*. The sheriff's bay, already standing splay-legged and wild-eyed, gave a snort and tried to pull from the rail. Tate lunged for the reins and snared the leather. "Whoa, goddamn you!" he cried in a frenzy of fear of the stamping, terrified animal. The smell of death was in the horse's nostrils, and it was all the banker could do to keep the animal from bolting. He jerked viciously on the reins, bringing sharp bit pressure to the horse's mouth.

It was an agonizing moment before it dawned on Tate what the problem was. He led the animal a few feet from the corpse. Once the horse could view the body from a distance, the panic seemed to abate. The bay came quickly under control and allowed the little man to lead it again up to the railing.

The remaining part of the task touched the last remnant of squeamishness left in Tate's makeup. But this was the most critical part.

Speaking softly to the bay, he lifted the sheriff's foot and tried slipping the entire boot, toe first, through the stirrup. The heel, though considerably worn down, prevented its passing. Tate was near frantic. He jerked the boot off, thrust the stockinged foot through the stirrup, and worked the boot back into place. The ridiculousness of what he was doing was lost in his frenzy. He glanced about, sweat streaming from his face into his eyes, saturating his collar.

He untied the wild-eyed bay and led it slowly from the hitch rack, away from the barn, its grisly burden dragging alongside.

Tate knotted the reins across the saddle, behind the horn. He considered this a moment, untied the reins, and let them trail on the ground.

When all looked right, he stepped to the animal's rear. His stringy gray hair hung in sweat bands before his eyes. He slapped the horse suddenly, emitting a shriek that first brought the bay back on its haunches and then propelled it forward like a cannon shot.

CHAPTER 23

AFTER Carrie's angry reproach, Tanner walked back to the Appaloosa, feeling angry and frustrated with himself—and suddenly quite lonely. Instead of stopping when he reached his horse, he continued on to the doors of the first saloon he came to. He badly needed a drink and a quiet place to hide. He pushed through the batwings into the cool interior and made his way directly to a back table—the same table, as it turned out, where he and Sams had split a bottle when Tanner had first ridden into Sweetwater. It was also the table where he and Reynolds had had an occasional drink. It seemed somehow appropriate to sit at the table one last time and ponder the ruin.

His thoughts of the sheriff made him wish Reynolds were here at this moment. Tanner simply lacked the volition to go out and look the man up. Also, it occurred to him that as he and Carrie had been arguing he had caught a glimpse of Reynolds from Doc's window, riding past, headed out of town. In the heat of the moment, he had not paid it much attention.

The bartender set a bottle before him. "Could you use one of these?" he asked with an understanding grin.

Tanner looked up gratefully. "You ought to take up mind reading, Loomis. Join me?"

Loomis walked slowly behind the bar and returned with another glass.

"You heard all about it, I suppose," Tanner said matter-of-factly as he poured.

"Workin' in a place like this, you got to ask me that?" Loomis was a thin man with a broad, angular face and a

164

pointed chin. He brought to the minds of many folks a picture of a walking shovel.

"Know where you're headed yet?" he asked in a commiserating tone.

"Ideas. Just ideas."

"You'll make out. You ornery ones always do. It's us righteous ones what suffer."

Tanner gave up a stoic grin and raised his glass. "Here's to all us ornery ones."

After a couple of drinks, the bartender moved back behind the bar and Tanner, surprising even himself, prepared to get down to some serious drinking. And why the hell not? It was all over but the shouting. All that remained was to ride out and pick up the last of his belongings. The horses remaining in the corrals he would simply turn free. With all the grass and running water around the place, Tate would have an easy enough time rounding them up when he wanted them.

He was on his fourth drink, beginning to relax nicely, when he heard the shouting and the gunfire.

The clientele at the bar and tables, Tanner included, rushed to the door. Everyone crowded around the batwings, necks craning, until it occurred to someone in front to push on through to the sidewalk.

A cowhand clutched the reins of a lathered horse while others were gathered about a ragged bundle suspended from the near-side stirrup.

"My God!" said someone. "It's Loyal—I think!"

"Are you sure? How the hell can you tell? The face . . ."

Tanner pushed through the swarm. One glance at the horse told him it belonged to Reynolds. The remaining shreds of clothing about the mangled body were the ones Reynolds had been wearing earlier in the day when he and Tanner had parted.

Tanner turned away, sickened. He didn't want to see any more. He reeled into a hitch rack and clutched at the rail for support. Behind him, voices buzzed like angry wasps.

"Make way!" someone ordered. "Open up so Doc can get in."

Brennan knelt in the dirt, black medical bag in hand. He saw at a glance it was hopeless.

"Get him out of that thing and take him over to my office," he instructed the suddenly subdued crowd. "I can't do nothing for him out here in the middle of the street."

Tanner watched, clinging to the hitch rail, as the limp form of the sheriff was trucked down the street and into the small, white-fronted office.

At some point, Davis, the deputy, had been summoned. Dazedly, he followed the parade behind the sheriff's body.

Five minutes passed before the deputy emerged, ashen-faced and shaken. A chorus of voices assailed him from the waiting cluster.

"I can't tell you a goddamn thing but what you saw with your own eyes," Davis declared hotly. "Sheriff's dead. Horse drug him to death, an' that's that." He spied Tanner and pushed his way free of the crowd.

He clasped Tanner's arm, almost brutally. "I got to talk to you," he growled, and pulled Tanner toward the sheriff's office.

Inside the quiet office, Davis dropped himself into the chair behind Reynolds's desk. Tanner felt a surprising pang of resentment.

Davis motioned him to the chair before the desk.

"Doc suggested I talk this over with you," he said finally, nervously lacing his fingers in front of him. "Doc don't think it was a accident. He couldn't figure how a man's boot with that high of heel could of worked its way through the stirrup at that angle. It could of happened, he says, but it ain't likely." He made a helpless gesture at Tanner.

Tanner tried to focus in on what the deputy was saying. "Reynolds was already dead—before the horse drug him?"

Davis shrugged. "Doc said could be. Another thing, the

back of the head was caved in like he'd been hit hard with somethin'."

Tanner thought a moment. "Could be it happened while he was being dragged."

"I thought of that too. But hell, Tanner, you seen 'im. He done most of that trip ridin' on his face. How'd he get the back side caved in? Looks to me like some amateur rigged it up to look accidental."

Tanner rubbed his eyes and sighed raggedly. "What are you going to do, Davis?" he asked wearily. The effects of the alcohol had worn off, leaving him feeling limp and washed out.

"I want to backtrack the horse. An' I want you to go with me."

Tanner pushed himself up. "Let's get to it."

The trail could not have been more plain had there been arrows pointing the way. They rode in silence, at an easy lope. Davis pointed out to Tanner that on the relatively smooth surface of the road the position of the body could have varied but little.

It appeared, as they deciphered the tracks, that the sheriff's bay alternately ran at a goodly clip, tired and slowed to a walk, and then was spooked or panicked on its own into flight once again. The trail showed no sign that the body had turned over or twisted so that the face was up.

"The way that foot was lodged into that stirrup, it would be next to impossible for the body to flip over," Davis reasoned.

Tanner did not respond. He was thinking about his last conversation with Reynolds, concerning John Tate's filly and Billy Tate. If Reynolds had ridden out to the Triple T for another look around . . .

Without warning he touched spurs to the Appaloosa, quickening the pace to a gallop. Davis cast a puzzled look in Tanner's direction and followed suit.

"I got a hunch" was Tanner's short reply to the deputy's questioning glance.

They ran the horses for a swift mile, walked for a minute, and then galloped on until the Tate ranch came in sight.

The dust had shifted somewhat, but the trail left by Reynolds's horse was still highly visible even at their quickened pace, though the riders scarcely glanced at it now.

They left the main road and stopped at a large white gatepost, beyond which began Triple T land.

On the right gatepost was a reddish smudge, low down, close to the ground. It showed up like a large blotch of rust against the stark white. Without dismounting, both men recognized the smear.

Tanner and Davis exchanged glances and rode on, the deputy glancing about nervously, Tanner intent and searching.

When they reached the ranch yard, John Tate's buggy stood before the house. The single bay horse waited in the traces, standing three-legged at the hitch rail. Though a new breeze lifting lazy plumes of dust about them wafted cool, sweat trickled down the face of Davis, and the men's shirts clung to their backs.

Davis glanced at Tanner uneasily as they walked their horses across the ranch yard. They dismounted and tied up next to the buggy.

A ghostly silence clung to the empty outbuildings and corrals. A single pony stood sleeping in a pen near the blacksmith shop, its mane ruffled by the breeze.

"Looks deserted," commented Davis, hitching up his gun belt, eyes ever searching.

"Tate's home," Tanner said, inclining his head toward the buggy. "You check in the house. I want to look around out here."

Tanner had noticed when riding in that the door to the stable was ajar. He directed his steps in that direction while Davis mounted the back steps of the house.

Tanner pulled gently on the barn door, and it swung outward on well-oiled, silent hinges. He hesitated a moment and then stepped inside. The stable appeared empty. Tanner heard a soft flutter of wings from a hidden corner high overhead, followed by a gentle *coo*.

He moved slowly down the center alley, right hand resting on his six-gun, stepping softly to mute the jingle of spurs. He glanced in each stall, right and left, as he went, knowing that if Billy or anyone else awaited him, he would be an open target.

Tanner traversed the entire length of the alley and was working his way back when he spotted a stain soaked into the clay floor of one of the stalls. Straw had been scattered in a haphazard attempt to cover the brown smear. He kicked aside the straw and found a larger patch of coagulated blood.

The wings above fluttered, and Tanner gave a start. He looked around quickly, but found he was still quite alone, only the whisper of the wind and a few dodging shadows caused by the light filtering in through the loose-fitting plank walls.

He kicked away more of the straw, and his foot struck something solid. Kneeling, he sifted through the matting until his hand closed around the handle of the hammer. He pulled back his hand, sticky with half-dried blood.

On his knees in the stall, Tanner thought to himself that the killer had probably planned on returning later for a more thorough cleanup job. He shook his head. Davis had been right. Whoever had committed the murder of Sheriff Reynolds had shown an amazing ineptness at disguising or obscuring the facts of the crime.

The head of the hammer was bloody, and the handle had lain in the pool of blood. Beyond question, Tanner knew this was the weapon used to kill Reynolds. Doc Brennan would have to testify to that if the case went to trial.

The rest must have happened pretty much as Doc Brennan had surmised, the murderer rigging the foot through the stirrup to make the death appear accidental. Again Tanner shook his head, rising and brushing the matted straw from his knees. He poked around a bit more until he was sure there was nothing else hidden. Then he picked up the hammer and walked from the stable.

His heart sagged as he walked up the stone walk toward the house. He passed Billy's knife-scrawled caricature of a man on the side of the whitewashed toolshed, and his mind returned to the evening he had walked into Billy's drawn gun. As he entered the Tates' ranch house through the back door, Charlotte met him.

"Mistuh Tanner, what's wrong? Why Mistuh Tate so upset?" She wrung her hands in the folds of her apron.

Tanner held the blood-caked hammer low at his side, out of the old woman's view, and moved past.

"We have a real problem here, Charlotte," he said as gently as possible. "Is Deputy Davis with Mr. Tate now?"

"They in the study. What's wrong?"

Tanner shook his head. "I just can't say now, Charlotte. I'm sorry." He moved rapidly from the kitchen, feeling an ache of pity for the old woman.

He found Tate and Davis in the study.

One glance at Tate told Tanner the banker was in shambles. His hair was awry. He sat at his desk coatless, in a shirt encrusted with dust and sweat. His tie was gone. There was an unhealthy flush to his cheeks, and he held a half-filled whiskey glass in both hands, too firmly, on the desk before him.

"Maybe you'd like to clarify what this idiot is trying to say, Lee." His voice was steady enough, but he held the whiskey glass with ever-whitening knuckles. "He's saying somebody on this ranch killed Sheriff Reynolds. I'm shocked, of course, that Loyal is dead. But what makes Davis think anyone here was responsible?"

For an answer Tanner dropped the hammer onto the desk. It slammed heavily, jarring Tate's whiskey glass. He watched

the banker's reaction. For a moment he feared the man
would swoon. The flushed cheeks turned waxy white. The
eyes closed and the lids fluttered spasmodically.

"John," began Tanner gently, "you're an intelligent man.
We don't need to play games. I found this in one of the stalls
in the barn. And a great deal of blood."

Tate opened his eyes and fixed them lifelessly on the
smeared hammer.

"Someone tried—someone made a very poor stab at making it look like an accident," Tanner said. "Tried to make it
look like Loyal's horse had drug him to death. But you know
that isn't what happened."

Tate shook his head and passed a hand over his eyes. The
man exuded alcohol.

"I don't know anything about it," he said faintly.

Tanner glanced at Davis. The deputy had taken a station
near the cold fireplace.

"John, where's Billy?" Tanner asked. "Where's your son?"

Tate looked up sharply. "See here, Tanner. Who the hell
do you think you are? You're not the law."

"Afraid you're wrong there, Mr. Tate," Davis said. "With
the sheriff dead, I'm actin' sheriff. I deputized Mr. Tanner
to help out."

"I want a federal marshal down here," Tate demanded. "I
don't recognize your authority."

"Are you really sure you want a marshal?" asked Tanner.
"Listen, I don't believe you killed the sheriff. But I think
you're the one who made such a poor try at covering it up.
Tell us where Billy is. Did he take that horse of yours and
make a run for it?"

Tate's eyes gleamed wickedly. "You leave my boy alone.
There's no way you can tie him to any of this."

"I think we can," Tanner answered. "Eventually. Loyal all
but tied that filly of yours into being at the scene when Troy
was killed. And he found her tracks at the fire at the Farley
ranch."

"There's no way you can trace that horse anywhere," Tate answered stoutly. "You go talk to Billy if you want. But, by God, unless you got some solid proof, you leave your hands off him! Or, so help me God, you'll be dealing with every man on this ranch! I won't allow my son to be locked up. You'll find Billy with Quince up north near the settlement. They're doing some gathering up there."

Tanner nodded at Davis, and they moved toward the door.

In the hallway they met Eleanor, descending the stairs. Davis walked on outside. She stared at Tanner blankly and then smiled.

"Why, Lee, how nice to see you. And where did you drop from?" A strange light danced in her lovely blue eyes.

"Eleanor, I'm sorry about all this," he said huskily. The sight of her on the staircase hit him like a hammer blow to the chest.

"Sorry about what, dear?" She circled her arm through his. "Listen, we must take another ride soon. It's been ages, and the weather has been so nice lately."

Tanner could only stare at her.

"Well, listen, darling. Daddy's expecting me. We have some last-minute details to take care of before the wedding." She reached up and kissed him on the lips. "You be good," she murmured. She turned and entered the study, closing the door softly behind her.

Tanner stumbled blindly for the door, his pulse throbbing painfully in his temples.

CHAPTER 24

TANNER and Davis circled the house and rode north, following what appeared to be a well-worn trail to the northern grazing sections of the Triple T.

In response to Davis's questioning, Tanner filled the deputy in on the scene in the stable; the bloodied stall, scattered straw, and blood-smeared hammer.

Following that, neither man seemed inclined to talk. They rode in silence for the next fifteen minutes until they encountered a rider, a young Tate puncher returning to the ranch on an errand.

"Billy? Yeah, Billy's out there. Workin' his butt off. Which is a gawdamighty miracle all by itself." The young man took off his hat and whipped dust from it on one chaps-encased leg. "Say, wouldn't happen to have the makin's, would ya?"

Davis tossed him the tobacco sack. "Keep it," he said, and they rode on.

Ten minutes later, they reached the settlement, a cluster of abandoned shacks. There was one large gathering pen, and it was here the herds grazing the northern sections were driven for branding.

Amid the bawling sea of whiteface cattle were cursing, shouting cowhands. The yellow dust was so thick it settled instantly over man and horse, clung to face and neck, crept into nostrils along with the smell of burning flesh and hair.

Tanner searched the sweat-blackened faces of the men until he spotted a slight figure bending over a struggling calf.

"That'll be him." Tanner indicated the figure with a nod, and approached the fire, threading his way between the charging horses and working, cursing men. Davis followed a half-step behind.

A grime-smeared, agonized face looked up as Tanner called his name.

"I'll be damned," said Billy Tate, straightening up and placing a knuckled fist to the aching spot over his kidneys. "I figured you'd have skulked out of the country by now."

He picked up a glowing TTT branding iron from the coals and slapped it against the calf's flank. Amid the smell of burning flesh and the bawling of the calf, he said loudly, "Now, I know the old man didn't invite you out here. Not these days. I don't think Eleanor did neither. And I know damn well I didn't. So just what the hell are you doin' here? Did you come out for our big showdown?" He grinned, and the dirt ring around his lips cracked.

"We're about to tell you, Tate," said Davis, inching closer to be heard above the din. "Come over here, away from the racket."

Billy looked strangely at the badge on Davis's chest, and then at Tanner. He stripped off his gloves. "Hold 'em up, boys," he called, and waved to the riders. "Have yourselves a smoke while I visit with the rabble here." He smiled, pleased at the few chuckles that followed him as he trailed Tanner and the deputy over to the fence.

"What's it about?" he asked, flexing his right fist against the stiffness in his fingers.

"You been here all day, Billy?" asked Davis.

"No. I got here about ten. Why?"

"Sheriff Reynolds was killed at your place today. Looks like someone beat his head in with a hammer."

Billy took an involuntary half-step backward. His look of shock seemed genuine to Tanner.

"Someone rigged it to look like his horse drug him to death," said Tanner.

"At my place, you say? You can't think I did it!" Billy's eyes narrowed, the bravado gone, replaced with a genuine note of fear.

"Sheriff had evidence you were in that gully when Troy Sams was murdered," Tanner lied. "And you were at the Farley place when it was torched. Reynolds was out in the stable checking on that little mare you were riding the night you passed me. The hoofprints matched up perfectly."

"I never rode that horse anywhere near the Farley place," Billy said, his voice rising in pitch, "or anywhere near where Troy was killed. You're playin' a get-even game, Tanner. Pa's runnin' you out of the country and you're just shootin' wild."

"Just a goddamn minute, Tate," spoke up Davis with a surprising note of authority. "Tanner came out 'cause I asked him—as a deputy. Now I ain't just exactly sure who done the killin', but God knows there's plenty around here to wonder about. Your pa looks like the tail end of a three-day drunk. Then there's the matter of you an' that horse." Davis was getting his steam up. His face was flushed under the dust, and a vicious forefinger jabbed at Billy's narrow chest. "An' the one thing we know for sure is Loyal Reynolds was killed in your barn!"

"I don't know nothin' about that!" declared Billy, next to panic. "And you can't prove a goddamn thing!" He jerked the leather thong from the hammer of his six-gun. "Now just what the hell are you goin' to do about it?"

As with most cowhands, the riders of the Triple T carried a sense of loyalty to the outfit. It mattered not whether the boss's son was right or wrong; they would back his play until the boss said different.

Davis knew this, and he nervously eyed the crew, beginning now to gather about. The looks on their faces made the deputy hesitate.

Tanner looked around at the grim faces. "I think your dad had the best idea," he said.

"Yeah? And what was that?" sneered Billy.

"He's for calling in a federal marshal to look into it."

"Federal marshal?" challenged a voice from behind. It was the foreman, Quince. "What the hell's going on here? Why is work stopped?" He glowered at Tanner. "Davis, fill me in," he growled.

"Sheriff was killed this afternoon," Davis answered. "Killed in the stable at the Tate ranch. We got reason to believe Billy here might know something about it."

"Billy's been here all day, right under my nose. Whoever your killer is, it ain't the kid."

"You ready to swear that in court?" asked Davis. "If it turns out he did it, you'd be in a mess of trouble."

"I'll swear it," answered the foreman with a surly glance at Tanner. "And so will the whole damn crew. We all been here together." He turned to Tanner. "You stirrin' this up, Tanner, because of Tate taking your ranch?"

Tanner started to reply. Davis cut in. "Fact remains, we got a dead sheriff an' we're goin' to find out who killed him. Tanner's only here 'cause I asked him. And I'll tell you men something else—we'll have your cooperation on this or you'll all be answerin' to the marshal yourselves."

"We ain't scared of no marshal," one of the men yelled.

"No?" Davis answered hotly. "How do you feel about the Army? Federal marshal has any trouble, that's who he calls for help. Any of you boys remember just how close we are to the fort?" He turned and slipped through the poles of the fence. "C'mon, Tanner. I got me a telegram to send."

They rode off, feeling angry eyes on their backs, and both breathed more easily when they had ridden out of rifle range.

"What do you think?" Davis asked finally.

Tanner shook his head. "Much as I hate to say it, the kid acted like he was telling the truth. Did you see how he reacted when he found out the sheriff was dead?"

"I saw it," Davis answered slowly. "But I had the feelin' something was there. Didn't you?"

"Like he didn't do it but might have an idea who did?"

"Right."

Tanner glanced at the sky. Heavy clouds were being pushed in from the southwest. A quick calculation of the light wind, and Tanner estimated they would just have time to make town before the storm hit. The sun was low, cradled in the western end of the valley.

As they rode in silence, Tanner reworked in his mind the circumstances, listing his questions, working for some kind of logical solution, or at least a clear understanding of each point.

He had been so certain that Billy had been actively involved in the murders. The kid had a dangerous chip on his shoulder. He classed himself good with a gun. With his father's wealth and influence, he might have figured the law would have a hard time reaching him.

The one thing that would not wash was the reason. What possible reason could Tate have for killing those men? Had he had bad feelings with those people—dealings no one knew about? And what had he against Loyal Reynolds? Tanner had lied to Billy, hoping for some reaction, when he had said the sheriff had evidence against Billy. All he really had was some tracks that quite likely would match up with those of the thoroughbred filly. There wasn't a hope in hell of proving that Billy had been in the saddle when those tracks were made.

A large warm drop of rain hit Tanner on the cheek. He blinked and looked up accusingly at the sky. The clouds had massed overhead much sooner than he had anticipated. A moment later, a stiff and sudden breeze drove more drops into his face. The sun had been snuffed out by a piece of gray cloud, and thunder rumbled in the west.

The ground over which they rode was slightly hilly, covered with grass that reached to their horses' knees. Ahead, but far to the right, was the Tate ranch house, a white skull floating on the green sea. They would pass by the house a good half-mile to the east.

Tanner's thoughts were on Eleanor, somewhere within the walls of that house. His heart ached. He felt bitter, accursed. Sams and Farley were dead, Carrie nearly killed. Now Reynolds. It was a damn good thing he was riding on. If his hanging around caused something to happen to Eleanor, he could not go on. Whatever had happened, whatever craziness had spoiled their lives together, he loved her. He—

A distinctively sharp and distant clap of thunder reverberated across the rolling valley floor. He heard Davis grunt and turned to see the deputy lifted from the saddle and tossed into the long grass.

Tanner vaulted from the saddle and dropped to the ground, gun drawn. Davis lay staring dreamily up into the sky, clutching his left shoulder as blood seeped between his fingers. Tanner knelt quickly beside him, and Davis looked up at him.

There was another slap of a rifle report. The deputy's horse snorted and ran off a few yards, burned across the rump by a bullet.

"It's heavy caliber," muttered Tanner, crouching low, searching off to the southwest. "A fifty, at least."

"Hell of a shot, whatever," said Davis, struggling to sit up. "I didn't see nobody." His voice was ragged, his face an ashen hue.

Tanner's eyes swept the landscape. "There he is." The gunman stood too far away to determine his features, but there was no mistaking his horse. "I'll be damned," muttered Tanner.

Davis collapsed back into the grass. Tanner made a quick inspection of the wound and found the bullet had gone completely through the upper part of the shoulder. The flesh was badly torn up, but, miraculously, the slug had missed all bones.

Keeping an eye on the gunman, Tanner fumbled a bandanna from his pocket and slipped it beneath Davis's shirt, over the gaping bullet hole.

"Press that tight," he instructed. "And relax, Davis," whispered Tanner. "It ain't that bad."

Davis opened his eyes and tried to grin. "Don't worry about me. You just make sure you take care of that bushwhacker."

Tanner nodded grimly. "I guess we ain't going to get a better chance. And without a rifle, we sure as hell can't sit here and wait for him to ride up on us. You be all right?"

Davis's chin moved weakly. "Maybe somebody heard the shots. Anyways, I can hang on until you get back. Just be careful, huh?"

Tanner got up from the ground warily. The Appaloosa stood a dozen yards away. Tanner needed his rifle, but to make a move for Jake was to invite a bullet. The gunman moved steadily closer, moving at a calm, unhurried walk, a slight figure resting on the back of the thoroughbred filly. They were, at Tanner's estimate, within two hundred yards.

Tanner glanced quickly at his own horse. He had to move. He could not hope to hit anything at this distance with his six-gun, and he was not about to stand waiting for that deadly rifle to pick him off.

The dark horse and rider walked on. Tanner could make out a few details now. The dark clothes were denim pants and jacket, a black hat, and something darker swathed about the head beneath.

The rifle was held across the pommel, and the rider sat easy, confident and deadly. The dark horse moved forward in light, powerful dancing steps.

Tanner cast a quick glance at his own rifle in the saddle scabbard. It was now or never. He moved off from his crouched position, making a run for the Appaloosa.

"Be careful," came Davis's loud whisper from behind him.

He ran crouched low, six-gun in hand. As he ran, he glanced at the rider. The rifle was slowly rising.

Tanner snapped a quick, wild shot, hoping to divert the rifle for just a few more seconds.

He reached the Appaloosa just as the big rifle roared. The spotted horse staggered, its front legs gave way, and it went down with a grunt.

Tanner stared, mouth open. "Jake," he murmured, unbelieving.

He looked up, confused, eyes burning. The dark horse and rider continued on their slow, measured death march, rifle returned to its rest across the saddle. The figure was closer now, perhaps a hundred yards.

"You son of a bitch," Tanner said softly. And then he screamed, "Goddamn you! You killed my horse!"

He lunged forward, jerked the rifle from the scabbard, and fell prone across the body of his horse, resting the rifle on the saddle. He levered a shell into the chamber and placed the sight bead almost casually on the rider's narrow chest. He squeezed off the shot, then watched the horror unfold.

The rider crumpled in the saddle. In the next instant, the filly pitched sideways, throwing the rider clear.

As the filly bucked and pitched, Tanner was on his feet and running toward the downed rider. His rifle lay where he had dropped it, at the side of his dead horse. He ran as a man who had been frightened to the very depths of his being. He feared not for his own life now, or for Davis's. He was praying as he ran that what he knew at this moment to be true might yet not be true.

As the rider had fallen, the hat had gone flying and a dark scarf about the head had slipped free, exposing blond hair. He found her on her back in the deep, soft grass. One small hand held weakly to a metal button on the jacket. Blood pumped through the hole in the denim in a steady, even course.

He knelt beside her. With a soft cry he lifted her, cradling her in his arms, her features blurred beneath his watering eyes.

"I didn't know," he moaned, holding her tightly, as if to press his own life into her.

Her eyes seemed fixed on his, unblinking, her features waxen, her smile frozen.

"Lee, darling," she murmured.

CHAPTER 25

IT was a warm, sunny Sunday morning when Tanner left the hotel and started out for the Tate ranch. He had placed his saddle and his light provisions on the buckskin, the little horse that had shown so much promise under Tanner's first ride. On his way out, he dropped by the sheriff's office to see Davis.

The deputy, still the acting sheriff, was sitting at the desk, drinking coffee and eating breakfast when Tanner entered. Davis's left arm was bound tightly to his chest, and his slow, careful movements indicated how sore the wound was yet.

"I'm pulling out this morning, Davis," said Tanner. "I just wanted to drop by and say so long and thanks for everything."

Davis rose from his chair and extended his good right hand.

"I'm sorry about all this, Tanner. Too bad things had to turn out so sour."

Tanner smiled grimly. "Well, there's always the next valley." He shifted restlessly on one foot. "I've got to make one last trip to talk to John Tate. From there, I don't know."

Davis nodded. "That might be a good idea. If you need to put a handle on this thing, that's the place to start." He moved his left arm, wincing. "Legally, there ain't a hell of a lot can be done to ol' John, even if a body was a mind to. Marshal Benton, he's got a kind heart. Kind of raked Tate over the coals for tamperin' with evidence, an' let it go at that." The deputy hesitated. "You sure you won't be stayin' in the valley?"

Tanner shook his head without speaking.

"There's one thing you better do," Davis said. He seemed reluctant. "You better say so long to Carrie. Without wantin' to come an' see you herself, she's been keepin' tabs on you. She knows you're hurtin', an' she's real concerned, Tanner."

"That's one meeting I'd better skip," said Tanner sadly. He turned slowly toward the door. He stopped and let out an exasperated sigh. "But you're right. I just can't leave without seeing her. Take care, my friend." They shook hands again, and Tanner left.

The Tate ranch was fairly serene and still. A few hands regarded Tanner sullenly, but one or two raised a hand at him as he rode in, dismounted, and tied the buckskin to a hitch rail.

He walked slowly up the front walk, his mind a stampede of memories of Eleanor. The hopes and the plans they had shared seemed like dreams from a long-ago childhood. He mounted the steps to the veranda and remembered the evening hours they had spent here. He knocked on the heavy door, and Charlotte answered.

Tanner was saddened at the way grief had ravaged the old woman. Her eyes seemed to throb with dull pain, and a new feebleness had taken hold of her frail frame. She moved haltingly to one side, beckoning him to come in.

"Mistah Tate's in the study. He spends all his time in the study now. Never went into the bank last week . . . not even onct." She clutched at his arm, and he looked down into eyes filled with pain. "What happen, Mistah Tanner? It don' make no sense to me."

Tanner placed a gentle hand on her thin shoulder. "I don't know, Charlotte. That's why I came out—to see if I could figure things out a bit."

Tanner turned to the study door, rapped softly. There was a soft response from within, and Tanner opened the door and stepped in.

It looked so natural, so very normal. John Tate sat behind his polished desk, wearing a black suit immaculate against a gleaming shirtfront, fingers laced together before him. The eyes looked tired, disinterested. And the folds of skin about the eyes and jowls hung a little lower.

"I'm glad you came, Lee," Tate said softly. "I thought of coming to see you. There's much we need to talk about before either of us finds peace in this thing. Please, sit down."

Tanner seated himself in the leather chair, the very one where he had sat while signing the purchase agreement for the Whiteman place. How different things had been then. The whole world had been at his feet. He had been so close to having everything a man could want.

Tate indicated the portrait of his wife behind Tanner. "I was just sitting here thinking about Eleanor, how she was so much like her mother in so many ways, except much sweeter. She needed so much love. And she needed to give love. But I guess Justine passed some of her selfishness on to Eleanor—enough that maybe it drove her a little mad."

"You knew about this all the time, didn't you?" Tanner demanded suddenly. "Why in God's name didn't you stop her?"

"You're wrong," Tate said. "I knew *after* the fact. Never before it. I swear it! I figured each time—with Bridges, then Troy—if I could just cover it up, that would be the last. That she would get better—I always hoped and prayed that she would get better." Tate wrung his hands helplessly. "I lost my wife, Lee," he said piteously, "I couldn't lose Eleanor, too."

"And so you let her kill four people?"

"When Quince brought you in," Tate continued, "you were like a candle in a dark room. And the more you were around her, the more Eleanor acted like her old self. Lee, you were a gentleman. You loved her, and I know for a fact she loved you. With you in the picture, I was sure it would at last be settled."

"If she loved me so much, why . . ." Tanner paused and

shook his head before going on. "I always suspected Billy because I saw him riding that damn horse. John, are you absolutely sure? I mean, the killings were done by someone good with guns. Could Eleanor really shoot that well?"

Tate smiled with bittersweet pride. "Since she was in her teens. In a way, you can blame all of this on old Rooster. He taught her to ride and shoot like a man. It was something she just took to. You know how she handled a horse. You've gone riding with her," he said proudly. "She handled guns just as well. She and Rooster would take different pieces from my relic collection and fire them. They're all functional. The weapon, the one she fired at you and Davis, was the Sharps. She could use them all equally well."

Tate continued speaking of his daughter in worshipful tones. That John Tate loved his daughter was without question. How healthy was that love was another matter.

Abruptly, Tate looked at Tanner. "We used you, Lee. I wanted to set up a ready-made, normal life for her. You were older than the rest, more settled in mind and purpose." He raised his hands helplessly. "It should have worked."

Tanner got to his feet slowly, like an old man in pain. "No, John," he said wearily. "It couldn't have worked. Not in a million years. You should've got help for Eleanor. As it is, you killed her just as surely as I did." He walked to the door.

"Lee," John Tate called out. "Stay. You can have your ranch back. It's all yours, Lee. Same deal as before. Or write your own deal. I want you to stay. Next to me, she loved you more than anyone else."

His hand on the door, Tanner looked back. "I got no need to live in a mausoleum, John. She would be everywhere I looked. I want to be free of those memories. Free of Eleanor."

"I understand," he said. "But please accept Venus as a gift, Tanner. It's the least I can do. . . ."

*   *   *

Tanner had one more stop to make before he could truly be free of Sweetwater and its memories. He rode out to the Farley place.

Carrie had left Doc's days ago and was staying with the McIntoshes, but she spent most days working at her ranch.

Her voice had worsened. Doc Brennan had told her about the scars on her vocal cords and had reassured her that she would not lose her voice altogether, but the damage was permanent.

Physically she was almost as strong and healthy as ever. When Tanner rode in leading the thoroughbred filly, Carrie had the stallion's near front hoof clinched between her knees, working with a rasp, smoothing the hoof in preparation for shoeing.

When the stallion saw the filly, it raised its fine head and whinnied.

Carrie released the hoof and straightened up slowly, rubbing the small of her back.

The stallion snorted and stamped, pulled at its tethered lead rope. The filly answered with a sharp squeal.

"It's like that, huh?" Tanner smiled and pulled the buckskin to a halt a good twenty feet from Carrie and the stallion. He tied the filly to a fence rail, then tied the buckskin to block off the stallion's view of the filly.

Carrie moved away from the excited stallion. She leaned against the pole fence with her elbows resting on a rail behind her. She looked relaxed and at peace.

Tanner walked up slowly, taking off his hat. "Hello, Carrie," he said, feeling clumsy. "You're looking fine."

Carrie smiled and acknowledged the compliment with a nod. She looked at the filly and then at Tanner questioningly.

"A little present for you. Tate insisted I take her. But hell, one horse is all I can handle right now. Tate's letting me keep the buckskin there. You know I lost old Jake?"

She nodded again and whispered, "It's kind of hard for me to talk. But it's nice to see you, Lee."

Their eyes held for a moment. "It's real nice to see you too, Carrie."

She looked away. He cleared his throat and moved around where he could lean against the fence next to her. Together they watched the horses.

She pointed at the house. Neighbors had pitched in on the rebuilding. "Nearly finished," she said.

As far as Tanner could see, all that remained to be done was installing window glass. It was a nice little home, about the same size as the one that had occupied the spot before, but better planned. And it was more appealing to the eye. There was a faint note of melancholy in the quiet little structure—Carrie Farley eating lonely, silent meals; waking up to a still, lonesome house.

Tanner looked down at her. She was gazing at the house with quiet eyes, as though she viewed the same gloomy scenes as Tanner.

She was tough, thought Tanner. She would never mention her fear at having to face the future alone. And without a single doubt, she would survive. Survive, yes, but would she thrive? Tanner did not think so.

Carrie jerked a small thumb at the young stallion, which stood striking the earth with a front hoof, rolling wild eyes in the filly's direction.

"Reminds me of a story," she tried in whispery tones. "Man sells his watch to buy his girl a comb for her hair. Finds out she sold her hair to buy him a chain for his watch." She gave a little choked laugh. "Who'd want a bald woman anyhow?"

Tanner looked at her curiously.

"I was going to give you that stallion," she explained. "I got no real use for him. Now you give me this filly . . ." Her voice cracked and she could not finish, but she looked up at him with eyes filled with dry humor.

"I see what you mean," he said, smiling. "But a man without a ranch or mares don't need a stud."

They stood for a time without speaking. Tanner felt he

should go, but was somehow reluctant, knowing at the same time that the longer he tarried the worse it would be.

"It wouldn't be fair to you, Carrie," he said abruptly. "You shouldn't have to take anyone's leftovers."

She seemed not to hear.

"I loved Eleanor," he went on, "whatever problems she might've had. And I wanted a life and a home and family with her. You shouldn't have to live in the shadow of that."

Her silence rankled him. He grabbed her by the shoulders and forced her to face him. Her eyes rose to meet his, proud and, he thought, maybe a bit scornful.

"Damn it, Carrie, I—"

"Hold it a minute, Tanner." Her voice was an agonized whisper, but her eyes crackled with anger. "No one's asking you to be a martyr. God knows we both got enough problems to deal with. But I'll handle mine just fine without you. Go off somewhere and lick your wounds. I'm stayin'." She mouthed more words, but no more sound came forth.

Tanner was glad her voice had given out. He smarted from the quick lashing she had given him. He used the chance to grumble, "I ain't trying to be a martyr. I'm just thinking what's best for you."

"Don't you dare say that! You might be thinkin' of yourself or Eleanor or John Tate or the drunk down the road. But, buster, you sure as hell ain't thinkin' of me. Just who the hell are you to decide what's best for me? You're not my father, although you might be old enough."

Despite his anger, Tanner almost smiled. They stared at each other for a moment.

"I know what's best for me. And," she added with a smirk, "you haven't done so good your own damn self anyways."

Tanner was on the point of a sharp reply when he realized what she had said was exactly right. He was no expert on this girl's—this woman's—life. He cared about her, and wanted her to make the right choices, but how did he know what the right choices were? His own life had not exactly been a raging success.

Carrie turned her back to him and stared at the stallion. Her throat ached, and she was not sure if it was from the strain of her outburst at Tanner or from the strain of what she was trying to keep from saying.

Tanner stared helplessly down at the young woman. Her face was shielded from his view by the battered brim of her hat.

He should go. It was time he should go. But damn her! Now he didn't want to. She had, in the span of less than a minute, destroyed his noblest of feelings. Five minutes ago, he could have ridden off feeling like a suffering saint. If he left now, he must skulk off like a coyote. *Damn it,* he thought.

"Damn it!" he said aloud, explosively, but with a broad grin. He tilted her chin up so he could see her face. "I've got to hear just one more word from you, Carrie. And then I don't give a damn if you ever speak again. But say it."

Carrie stared up at him intently, a soft smile in her wide eyes.

"Say it," he repeated, now pleading.

"Stay," she whispered.

IF you have enjoyed this book and would like to receive details of other Walker Western titles, please write to:

Western Editor
Walker and Company
720 Fifth Avenue
New York, NY 10019